FLIGHT
from the
FORTRESS

Fitzhenry & Whiteside, 195 Allstate Parkway,
Markham, Ontario L3R 4T8

In the United States,
121 Harvard Avenue, Suite 2, Allston, Massachusetts 02134

www.fitzhenry.ca   godwit@fitzhenry.ca.

10 9 8 7 6 5 4 3 2 1

National Library of Canada Cataloguing in Publication

Cook, Lyn, 1918-
Flight from the fortress / by Lyn Cook.

ISBN 1-55041-790-8 (bound).–ISBN 1-55041-792-4 (pbk.)

1. Louisbourg (N.S.)–History–Juvenile fiction. I. Title.

PS8505.O66F45 2003   jC813'.54   C2003-902339-7
                      PZ7

U.S. Publisher Cataloging-in-Publication Data
(Library of Congress Standards)

Cook, Lyn.
Flight from the fortress / Lyn Cook.—1st ed.
[   ] p.: cm.
Summary: In 1713, the British and French battled in a winner-take-all war for the Fortress of Louisbourg. A French boy comes looking for his English father, where he meets a young girl caring for two orphaned infants. They flee the fortress and to find refuge in the forests beyond.
ISBN 1-55041-790-8
ISBN 1-55041-792-4 (pbk.)
1. Louisbourg (N.S.) _History _ Juvenile fiction. 2. Nova Scotia _ History _ 1713-1763 _ Juvenile fiction. 3. Interpersonal relations – _ Fiction _ Juvenile literature. (1. Louisbourg (N.S.) _History _ Fiction. 2. Nova Scotia _ History _ 1713-1763_ Fiction. 3. Interpersonal relations _ Fiction.) I. Title.
[Fic] 21   PZ7.C665Fl 2003

Fitzhenry & Whiteside acknowledges with thanks the Canada Council for the Arts, the Government of Canada through the Book Publishing Industry Development Program (BPIDP), the Ontario Arts Council and the Government of Ontario through the Ontario Media Development Corporation's Ontario Book Initiative for their support for our publishing program.

Printed in Canada

Design by Wycliffe Smith Design Inc.

FLIGHT
from the
FORTRESS

By
LYN COOK

Fitzhenry & Whiteside

dedicated with gratitude
to all those who made it possible
for Fortress Louisbourg
to rise again
and to those who, every year,
make it a living presence;
and always,
for Kerry and Matthew

TO SET THE SCENE

The Fortress of Louisbourg, now one of the most beautiful and exciting living museums in Canada, began in 1713 at the end of the European War when France gave up its settlements in Newfoundland and Acadia to Britain.

The French King Louis XV ordered a new walled fortress built on Isle Royale, now Cape Breton Island, as a guardian of the oceans between Old and New France and a possible launching site for an attack on British New England to the south.

With its large, sheltered harbour and an ocean teeming with codfish, it grew to be a busy and profitable trading centre, necessary goods and supplies coming by sailing ship from Quebec, New England and the West Indies, in exchange for the codfish.

In 1745, New Englanders laid siege to the town and it became a British possession. All the citizens, except those who fled to the outports or the wilderness, were forced to return to France.

In 1749, the fortress was ceded back to France by treaty and once again, the streets were alive with French language and culture.

But Louisbourg was doomed. The British wanted it destroyed as the first step in their gaining complete control of the new colony in Canada. It fell to the attackers in July 1758.

I first saw the site of the fortress many years ago. It consisted then of mounds of rubble, the remains of stone foundations and a gray museum. Beyond, waves crashed on the Atlantic shore, sending showers of spume into the salty air. In 1961, Parks Canada began to rebuild the fortress as a national historic site. When you go there and see the citizens, the fishermen, the merchants, soldiers, innkeepers, the nobility with their families and servants, attired in the clothing of their day, going about their daily business, you will have stepped back in time, to the year 1744. Perhaps Philippe, Gaby, Jonas, the Monk and all the others will be there, just as they were when the fortress was nearing its downfall. Remember them.

Remember, too, that I owe a great debt of gratitude to all those who have written about or guided the fate of the fortress, most of all to Eric Krause, the retired architect of Louisbourg, who sent reams of material, photos and a bibliography of required reading and to Bill O'Shea, Head of Historical Research, who fully explained the structures of the wall defences and other details. These were invaluable to my living the lives of my characters in the story. My gratitude is not diminished by the few liberties I have taken with times and places. Christopher Moore's *Louisbourg Portraits* holds a special place in my acknowledgements for more than its excellence. Upon returning from an RCAF (WD) Reunion in Halifax, I brought my late husband the book as a gift. His delight in it is a fond memory.

My appreciation also includes the Royal Ontario Museum whose specialists provided me with splendid detail about the flora and fauna of Cape Breton, the French Isle Royale, just as they did so willingly for my previous novel, *The Hiding Place*, and its setting in New France.

I add abundant thanks to my editor, Laura Peetoom, for a firm hand on content and syntax, to Robert Sutherland, fellow-author, for timely encouragement, and to my dear friend, Wendy Laviolette, who, chapter by chapter, shared the manuscript with me while preparing it for publication.

May your time-travel to the Fortress of Louisbourg, just before its fall in 1758, be filled with new sights and sounds and, above all, with adventure!

CONTENTS

1
Rescue!
2
The Hole in the Wall
3
A Secret Shared
4
The Mysterious Monk
5
A Runaway in the Dark
6
Flight to the Forest
7
A Body in the Water
8
The Cry in the Night
9
"Stop or I'll Shoot!"
10
A Strange Gift of Food
11
The View From the Cliff
12
The Rage of a Storm
13
The Figure Between the Rocks
14
A Reunion – and a Surprising Encounter
15
Shadows
16
Journey into Darkness
17
"Fair blows the wind for France!"

Rescue!

Fool! Fool! Come back! You'll drown! Philippe longed to shout the words into the darkness. He knew he could not. If he didn't stay silent and hidden he could lose his life to a swift shot from the sentry walking the fortress ramparts.

The blaze of battle had flared on the far horizon as he'd found shelter in a sod-covered fisherman's hut on the beach. It was while he was peering out, searching for a furtive entry to the massive fortress walls that Philippe had seen the girl and her boat in the water. The small cove was just out of sight of the sentry, who intermittently stalked the ramparts, but it was still too close for complete safety.

Why was she there? It was sheer folly, with the town under attack and the waves so treacherous to venture at midnight beyond the protection of the walls. What was he to do, watch helplessly while she drowned, or risk betraying his presence to those guarding the shore? Suddenly he had no choice. Her boat capsized beneath a mammoth wave. The girl disappeared.

Philippe's response was instant. He plunged into the fog and icy water and swam with wide, deep strokes to where the swirling depths had sucked her down. When she resurfaced, Philippe was ready. Grasping her long hair in one of his hands, he propelled them both furiously with the other, struggling to keep their heads above water. He felt the rocky shale beneath his feet. He knew they had made it to safety.

He hauled his burden up on the pebbly shore and caught one swift glimpse of an oval face, deathly white with exhaustion and fear, and a mass of tangled, dark hair. Then he knew no more.

He was dimly conscious of his body roughly shaken and a child's urgent whisper, "Massa! Massa! Réveillez-vous! Sentry! Sentry!"

He tried to clear his head of water and looked up into a small black face close to his own. A slave! Perhaps he was from one of the households near the quay. But where was the girl Philippe had rescued? He struggled to sit up, and stared around. There was no sign of her.

"Massa! Entendez! Come!" The child was almost in tears.

"Lead!" Philippe whispered, "Je suive!"

Silently, crouched to the ground, they made their way past a massive, closed gate. They seemed to be circling bastion walls. In a ditch below, water gleamed. They passed a sturdy closed door. Almost invisible in fog and darkness, close to the sloping, surrounding ground, was a small hole in the wall.

"There!" the slave boy pointed.

A hiding place! Philippe crept in, and at once the slave boy began to pile up stones in front of the entrance.

"But how did you know I needed a place to hide?" Philippe asked softly.

The child answered Philippe's French with an unintelligible gabble of his own. Then he broke into English, obviously his language of choice, still in a whisper. "I watching! I always watching!" And what secrets a young slave, considered of no importance, could easily discover as he ran errands for his owners!

Philippe reached out to try to grasp the boy's hand. "But what about the girl? Where is she?"

There would be no answer. The boy was gone. But Philippe had a place to hide, thanks to the young slave.

Had the boy made the hole or had the constant damp and fierce storms done their work on crumbling mortar, aided perhaps by the British attack on the fortress thirteen years earlier? Who cared? This was a place to hide and rest and make plans.

Philippe finished covering the entrance with the stones and small boulders. Then he felt secure. What was the hard shape in the hole pressing against his leg as he curled up? A small hessian sack filled with scraps of food and a chisel-like tool. The slave boy must have seen him crawling along the beach to the fisherman's hut and guessed his need. But why was the boy watching at all?

Hunger drove all questions from his mind. Ravenous, he fell on the food. Little wonder. He had trudged miles overland from Acadia on the sparsest of rations. Fishermen on the water between the island and the mainland, farmers, even a young Micmac had fed and sheltered him when they learned he was searching for his father. Language had not been a problem. With a French mother, wooed and won by his English father in the wars abroad, Philippe spoke both languages fluently, even a little Micmac if circumstances demanded it.

He recalled his first sight of the fortress at the end of his long journey. The place was built on a spur of land jutting out into the wild Atlantic, even the protected harbour open to all the raging ocean gales. A rare shaft of sunlight had lit the stone buildings crouched behind the massive walls, pointing heavenwards, the spire in the bastion of the Governor's residence.

And walking the town streets while disguised as one of its citizens, was his father, Richard Wyndham, his mission to spy on the French defences. His father could survive anywhere. Philippe knew that. Like himself, Richard Wyndham was fluent in both languages but also cunning and resourceful. If only he could know his father had entered the town safely, undetected as an enemy. It was his constant hope and prayer.

Uninvited, his thoughts turned to concern for the safety of the girl after her near drowning. But Philippe could not let that interfere with his reason for being there, his search for his father.

His hunger satisfied and feeling secure in his hidey-hole, he drifted into sleep, wondering all the while about the girl. But it was confused images of his father that haunted his sleep and his sudden waking. He must make plans to creep out of the hole when night came again. Slipping unseen in the foggy dark, he could learn the layout of the town and then chance a venture later in daylight, moving with assurance like one of its own. He wrung out his clothes as best he could and tried to find comfort in the hole and the chillingly damp June weather. He curled up and slept again, lulled by the roar of the heavy surf.

He awoke abruptly and completely, his mind already on the problem of where it was the slave boy had brought him. Flexing his stiffened muscles, he tried to picture the map of the fortress his father had studied night after night and committed to memory before he set out on his mission. Philippe recalled the gleaming water in the ditch past which the slave boy had led him and the two steps descending to it. The huge door.

Then he knew. *The postern tunnel! He was in an outside wall of a postern tunnel!* His father had explained how these occurred at various points under the huge fortress walls to allow the citizens of Louisbourg easy entry to and exit from their fortress town. His father had pointed out how the passageways curved, snakelike, to prevent their being an easy target for armoured attack. If Philippe was careful, it should be possible for him to go through the tunnel himself to enter the town. With his fluent French he could meet any challenge. And he doubted if his ragged clothing was much different from that of many ordinary citizens who had done without so much for so long. But exhaustion had dulled all his senses. To the sound of firing, again he slept.

It was light when he woke and heard a high whining wind. He was hungry. Well, he'd been hungry before and likely would be again. Even scraps would be hard to find beyond the wall with the town under siege. He spent the day between sleeping and waking. When dark finally came, carefully he moved the stones to permit his exit, then replaced them. Clinging to the tunnel wall, he sidled along it. The ditch water shone dully below him. Then he was at the door.

Should he open it and enter? Who might be on the other side? He had no choice; he had to get into the fortress. The door opened easily, noiselessly. He shut it behind him and ventured on, keeping close to the inside tunnel wall. Ahead was a decided curve. *What lay beyond it? A sentry? A citizen? Surely at this time of night the people of Louisbourg would be asleep in their beds, not wanting to leave the safety of their town.* He listened. A murmur of voices. Soldiers, probably, manning the great fortress walls overhead. But not in the tunnel. The voices were too distant for that. He took a deep, trembling breath and rounded the corner. There was no one there. Darkness was all. But he could see the end door outlined by faint light. Did that mean there was someone beyond it or was it merely a glow from lanterns somewhere on the streets inside? He listened. There was no more sound, not even the voices. Cautiously he opened the door. He shut it again quickly.

A band of soldiers, some staggering with weariness, were making their way into a recessed entrance, perhaps to a barracks. He'd have to be extra careful. He opened the door a crack and peered out again. They were gone. There was no one in sight. He shut the tunnel door quietly, then slipped along the fortress wall, keeping close to the cold stone. He could hear nothing above his head. He'd have to take a chance to gain the town streets. Squirming on his stomach, he made his way down the incline away from the wall and came to what appeared to be a limekiln. Scarcely breathing, he crawled across an area of grass and rutted ground until a building loomed. Sidling silently along the building wall, his feet felt cobblestones. A street and houses! Even in the dark, he could see some were log caulked with moss and clay, some half timber, half stone, a good deal fancier than the fisherman's deserted sod hut where he'd taken shelter.

Then he heard the noise. *Was someone following him?* He melted into the darkness of a recessed doorway. The noise grew louder – tramping feet! *More than one person then!* Was this the moment of discovery? Would he be caught and accused of spying? But why should he fear? If anyone questioned him, he could always plead hunger and the need to find food for his siblings living on some back street. Hundreds of soldiers had been imported into town for its defence, and in days of war and uncertainty, citizens had come from outlying settlements seeking shelter here.

There was no time to run now. From his shadowed shelter he saw them. They were rounding what appeared to be a warehouse down by the quay. A platoon of soldiers, coming from guard duty. Their feet shuffled over the cobbles with an exhaustion so great they wouldn't be searching the shadows. They wore the uniforms of a Swiss regiment, red coats and striped vests. Some of the hired soldiers then, paid to come and defend the town. They passed like the shadows that hid him, faintly whispering their relief at being away from the ramparts for a few hours. How many would live to see the end of the siege? Only God knew that.

When the last soldier straggled out of sight, Philippe set off again, groping his way along building walls towards the quay. The stink of fish was everywhere. It was a town that depended on the cod fishery, but he knew little fishing would be done these days. The British fleet was in Gabarus Bay, the French fleet in the harbour, and a blockade of the harbour in place for weeks.

Then he smelled something else. Tobacco! Bales of it piled high against the warehouse wall. *Another sound!* He dove behind two huge bales, heart pounding. Something scuttled across his feet. A rat, in search of food. He crept forward inch by inch, keeping to the shadows. A row of barrels lined the quay. Molasses, he could smell it, and rum, both come from faraway islands in trade for cod. But now, like the tobacco bales, the barrels were a barricade against gunshot.

Out of the darkness a girl appeared, the one he'd rescued, he was sure of it! There was something about the slender body, the colour of the cloak. Without warning she turned to look directly at him. It was the same girl! The oval face, the long black hair wreathing the edges of the cloak hood! She'd seen him! His heart hammered. He waited for her to betray him. She walked on softly, without hesitation, and disappeared into the night.

But what was that behind her? A figure clothed entirely in white. Surely a monk in monk's robe and hood. But of what monastic order? The figure approached and paused, the face hidden by the hood. Then he was swiftly gone, gliding up the cobbled street like a ghost. *Was he a ghost? The way the figure walked, as if its feet had no contact with the cobbles, and the robe and hood itself, a sudden shape formed of mist in the night….* His grandmother in France believed in apparitions. She'd seen them herself, his mother had told him. *Could it be someone, back from the other world, who'd been killed in the first siege thirteen years before?*

17

A warning of things to come?

Philippe shivered. These were idle imaginings. He'd best get back to his hiding place and consider his next move, ghost or no ghost. He made a detour that brought him to the immense building forming one of the bastions. It was long and well constructed, like a castle on a rising slope.

"You there! What are you doing here?" The sentry's French words exploded from the guardhouse.

His answer was swift. "Looking for food, sir."

"Well, you won't find it here. This is the Governor's residence, the King's Citadel." He glared at Philippe suspiciously. "Are you new here?"

His heart beating fast, glibly he replied, "I've come from an outport to see what's going on." That at least was no lie. "We hear only rumours along the coast."

"You'll hear more than rumours later, when the real battle starts." The sentry's intense stare made Philippe tremble. "You're better off out of here. Get on your way." Philippe did that quickly, deeply relieved that the sentry had not doubted his story. So far all was well. He returned the way he'd come, keeping to the protection of building walls and the night shadows. Thank God there was no one near or in the tunnel. It was evident the fortress was concentrating all its defences where the town met the harbour and the sea.

Carefully he removed the small boulders hiding the hole's entrance, crawled inside and built the stones up after him. But there was a pressure against his leg. Another bag! Food! God bless that slave boy! Putting his own life in danger! Philippe ate hungrily bread and peas, scraps of meat still clinging to a bone, probably taken from the master's own household, even from the plates that ended up in the scullery. But food it was and that set before the fortress' governor couldn't have tasted better.

When he'd finished he realized with a pang of guilt that he'd probably eaten the boy's own meal. How could he ever make it up to the slave? He'd find a way somehow. Undoubtedly there were a number of slaves in town but he'd never forget that small anxious face with the beseeching eyes. In his ongoing search of the fortress, their paths would cross again, he was sure. Comforted and fed, he slept.

The Hole in the Wall

He wakened again to confused shouts and the pounding of
feet along the walls. What if a British shell hit the very wall
that hid him? But surely that was more likely on the harbour
front of the town. His hidey-hole was on the landward side,
away from the harbour. He peered out of it. The fog was there
again, thick as before. Should he take a chance and go down
to the harbour to see what was going on? It would be worth
it.

Silent as a shadow, he crept from the tunnel and moved
towards the quay. A battle was on in the bay. British ships
ranged close to the shore but the French batteries took them
on and with shouts and confusion, the British retreated to
deeper water. One was grounded. He could hear screams of
agony as wounded bodies fell from its decks into the water.
Philippe had no wish to be caught in this crossfire. Still with
no one on his path, he crept back to his hole, glad to huddle
in safety. What should he do now?

He was ravenous again, and thirsty, but he would have to
wait till night and try to find his own food. Then he'd search
for a way to be absorbed into the town's life so that food and
water would be available, and his search made easier.

Just after dusk he heard the whispering. He thought he
was dreaming since he'd spent the day dozing. But no! There

were voices, muted and mysterious, conversing in treasonous French.

"We won't last much longer. And once the British set foot on the beaches, we're done for!"

"What about the reinforcements from France?"

"The plague is working for the English there — so many sailors killed off, even the home fleet isn't up to scratch."

"There's nothing left for me here, anyway, even if I survive the battle. You know that, Jacques."

"Don't give up hope. There may be a way yet."

"The only way I want is a way out."

"Well, let's see if we can find one then. It's a risky business but we can try."

"It'll be riskier if the British make it ashore. We could even starve to death before that, and I can't do a thing about ..."

In the mumbled whisper, Philippe could hear despair.

The one called Jacques went on speculating. "I guess what's out there can't be worse than life here. Our uniforms are in rags, barracks running with lice and vermin, always half-starved."

"We could try to get through this postern wall. It isn't as thick as the fortress wall and it's close to the swamp."

Philippe held his breath. Surely they could hear his heart beating, as he could hear their whispers.

"If we could make it to the other side, we could watch for the sentry. He might be keeping an eye on the tunnel entrance. When he's out of sight, we'll go down the slope and through the palisade. I've got a good sharp knife to deal with that."

"We need a hole large enough for us to crawl through. And let's be sure there's fog when we try it. Come on, there must be some place along here where the salt and wind have crumbled the mortar on the outside."

Now what was he to do? What explanation could he give for hiding like a fox in a den? His breath was so tight, his throat hurt.

"Hey! Look here! These stones move easily! It could be a hole made by the last siege and never mended."

It was all up with him then. He squeezed himself into a ball hoping desperately to become invisible. He watched in horror as the stones from the inside of the wall were removed and light filtered through. He caught a swift glimpse of piercing blue eyes and a face, square and rugged.

The muted voices began again. "I'd never get through that. I'm too big. And this is too close to the Dauphin Demi-Bastion for safety. We'll have to keep away from those bastions. They're crawling with sentries."

"We don't have to report for duty yet. Let's try to find some part of the wall broken by the British shelling."

There was silence, then the one he now knew as Jacques whispered again. "Look, I'm beginning to wonder if it's such a good idea for both of us to go together. We'd be spotted more easily that way. Why don't we plan for you to go alone first and wait for me at the old limekiln. Before I come, I'll try to persuade …"

The voice faded. *Persuade whom?* Philippe didn't care, they were gone. Still trembling, he sank back against the hole stones. What a narrow escape! In future, he must follow the deserting soldiers' example, and keep away from those bastions, the main defences of the town, the great walled and armed projections at intervals along the length of the fortress walls.

His heart had slowed its beat and he curled up to keep warm and preserve his strength. He slept a long while, exhausted from hunger and stress. It was pitch black when he woke again and there was silence. Attacker and defender were preparing for an assault on the day to come. But what was he to do?

Then he heard the sound on the inside wall of the tunnel. Tapping! Gently, almost like some animal! An animal here? Impossible! The deserting soldiers returned in hopes of enlarging the hole? Well, the game was up then. Philippe, breathless, awaited his fate. Strangely, into his waiting, came a faraway echo of chanting, swelling and fading by turns in the night fog. Citizens on their knees in the chapel, praying for deliverance from the enemy? He, too, prayed, silently and fervently.

The tapping ceased. Mesmerized, he watched. The largest stone blocking the entry slowly moved. Wildly he sought an opening phrase, an excuse for his being there. A small black face peered in at him. The slave! The slave boy had come back to him! He heard the urgent command. "Massa! *Suivez! Vite!*"

Clutching his meagre belongings, Philippe scrambled out of his hiding place, replaced the stones and trod swiftly on the boy's heels. Once on the streets they were enveloped in fog and the harsh crump of shelling. The noise of renewed battle had brought people out of doors. Citizens of all classes, merchants in their elegant breeches and vests and fine knee-length coats, their wives in brocade, the humbler folk in coarse durable unbleached linen and rough wool, all mingled with soldiers. They questioned one another, seeking assurance or a safe shelter from the growing bombardment. As he sped, unnoticed, through the fog and clusters of people, Philippe wondered how many of the simply clad folk were fishers from Brittany, Normandy or the Basque country who came across the ocean every year for the cod and now were, like him, prisoners of the siege.

The war was in their midst and the acrid stench of burning was in their nostrils as they came upon two houses, destroyed by a British shell. On the cobbles lay the tattered remains of a wig once worn by some proud merchant. Curtains of crimson velvet, desks of finest mahogany and portraits framed in gold lay in the scorched ruins. God only knew if their owners, the rich merchants of Louisbourg would ever possess their like again, or even have such fine stone and timber dwellings in this place.

Suddenly, on a back street, hidden and quiet, the slave boy stopped. He knocked in rhythm on a house door. It opened quickly and the boy was gone. Philippe was inside a log house, a fire flickering on the hearth. The girl he'd rescued stood before him.

"Come to the fire," she ordered in her native French. "I'll fetch you dry clothes." She waited to see if he understood, as chilled to the bone he moved to hold his hands to the flames. His clothes had never dried from the night of the rescue. His whole body ached with weariness, his stomach with hunger.

Searching in a hand-carved wardrobe against the far wall, the girl found coarse woollen breeches, a knee-length coat of the same brown fabric, a shirt of unbleached linen, heavy hand-knitted socks and wooden sabots. "Put them on in the little scullery." She indicated a narrow cupboard off the main room. As he did her bidding, he passed two children, only babies, surely not more than one or two, huddled together in sleep on one of the narrow beds.

His old clothes, tattered and torn in places, she took as he came out and draped close to the fire. Then she beckoned him to a rough wooden stool and placed a bowl of hot soup in his hands. Beside it, on a pewter platter was a slice of bread smeared with fat. "Hog's lard is all we have left," she said, "and precious little of that."

Remembering his manners, he tried not to gulp the soup. The thick broth warmed him, body and heart. "Why are you so kind to me?" he asked. "You don't know me."

Her oval face glowed. "I know you saved my life. And you speak our language." She refilled his bowl from the pot simmering over the flames. "Eat now. We can talk later."

As he ate, he glanced around the simple log room with its shining cobblestone floor, folding pine table, two wooden benches, two chairs, and the wardrobe, all hand-carved.

"You have a cosy home here." He was remembering the long cold nights of his journey, sleeping in ditches and tree hollows, longing for a warm hearth.

"My father cut the trees from the forest to build it for us, and built it well. It protects us from even the most terrible winter gales."

He could see by the glowing candlelight that the blankets and quilts on the two beds were patched on almost every surface. No luxury here. But what was she doing wearing a dress of faded damask?

She saw the look, and guessed at his question. "It's from a wedding dress sent from France for one of the merchant's daughters. Jonas found it in one of the shelled and abandoned buildings and knew I could make something of it. I even had some left over for the babies' clothes."

"Jonas?"

"The slave boy who brought you here. He's a true friend of mine. He finds us food from the leftovers of the merchants' and traders' houses." She looked deeply troubled. "But how long can that last with a siege on and a battle raging? Everybody will be looking for the last crumb!"

A knocking came, loud and imperious, on the door. She didn't hesitate. With a whirlwind movement she gathered up his old clothes and shoved them and him into the wardrobe. He strained to hear her speaking.

"Ah, Monsieur Dutot, you're out late tonight. Are you anxious to see how the battle goes?"

"I thought I heard voices. I wanted to make sure all is well here."

"All is well, Monsieur, as well as it can be with the British battering our walls."

Philippe heard the splat and sizzle of the man's spittle landing in the flames.

He peered through the wardrobe door. The visitor was a big, thickset man, his face ugly and florid. His voice grated when he spoke. "The British! Pah! I'd like to knife every man jack o' them! They'll never take this town. We'll destroy every soldier and sailor who sets foot on French territory." He paused. "What did I hear then?"

"I was soothing the babies — perhaps that was it. You'd best get home now, Monsieur. Tomorrow will bring challenges for all of us."

There was a muttered reply. The door opened and closed. She waited, listening, then drew Philippe back to the fire, rearranging his clothes to dry.

"A friend of yours?" he asked.

"A friend of mine? Not of mine, nor of anyone's I think."

"Who is he, then?"

"Monsieur Dutot, the shoemaker. He's been employed by some of the richest men in town. He pretends to be my friend but he has a long nose and it's into everybody's business. He's a troublemaker. He betrayed two army deserters and they were shot."

Philippe said quietly, "He hates the British."

"He has reason. His small son was killed in the last siege by the British thirteen years ago, so you'd best be careful. You don't belong here, I know that, of course. Do you want to tell me where you came from?"

He stared at the fire, saying nothing. *Would she betray him or throw him out if he told the truth?*

She touched him briefly on the shoulder. "You're very tired. Why don't you sleep now and leave explanations till the morning?" She turned down the woollen blanket on the bed. "You'll have my place."

"No! Where will you sleep?"

"In with the little ones. There's still room. Wherever you've come from, you're worn out, I can see that."

He lay down. "How can I ever thank you?"

"You already have. You saved my life." She drew the blanket around his shoulders and went into the scullery to prepare for bed. When she came back, he watched, already half asleep, as she moved in her white gown to the other bed. Even as she knelt quietly in prayer beside it, he remembered that other figure in white, the ghost, and wondered again who he was. Then, overcome with exhaustion and his long journey, he slept.

A Secret Shared

He woke in the still dark. Had there been more knocking at the door? He hid under the blanket and waited. Monsieur Dutot again? The girl was exchanging whispers with another voice that sounded familiar. Then all was silent. Stupefied with exhaustion, he slept again.

This time he was wakened by the boom of firing and a gentle tap on his shoulder. "If you wake now, you can eat again. That'll give you strength."

He staggered out of bed to the stool and a bowl of porridge. The girl held up a large loaf of wheaten bread and a small measure of meat. "Jonas hasn't forgotten us!"

"Was that Jonas at the door?"

"Yes. He finds as much as he can for us in the dark. Without him we'd never have lived."

"I wouldn't have either." The food was a banquet to him. "Who owns Jonas?"

She gave him a wry smile. "Monsieur Dutot. He got him in exchange for a fine pair of boots from a merchant trader on a British ship. That's why his French is a little odd and all mixed up with English. He comes from the West Indies."

"How can a British ship trade here when France and England have been at war for years?"

"Oh, there are ways. Many an official in town is persuaded to turn a blind eye if there's a little bribe offered."

Philippe hid his excitement. Was this how his father had come ashore? He tried to sound casual. "Where do the British ships come from?"

"Mostly from New England, the British colonies to the south of us. We depend on everybody else just to keep us alive, grain from Quebec, sugar and rum from the West Indies, and building materials, livestock and ships from New England. With the harbour blockaded, we're poor orphans."

He had to find out where his father might have landed. "Where do the ships sail into port?"

"There are a lot of small harbours and settlements along the coast of Isle Royale. Ships could put in anywhere. Anywhere that is, they could get the codfish they came for."

"I could smell the cod down on the quay when I went there."

"You can smell it all over town but we get used to it. Fishing begins as soon as the pack ice moves away from the shore. After all it's where our living comes from. Came from," she amended suddenly. She sat on the floor beside him and looked down at her hands. "What am I to do with these now, to keep us alive? My father was a fisherman."

Philippe frowned. "Was?"

The two children woke and began to whimper for care and food. She rose to tend them, his question unanswered. Washed, dressed and fed they came, one walking, the other crawling. They examined him, wide-eyed. "This is our new friend," the girl said gently. She turned to him, with a half-smile. "Here we've been discussing the affairs of the world and I don't even know your name."

He had to trust his life to her. He had to answer honestly. "Philippe Richard Wyndham."

"You're British. I thought you were, even with your perfect French."

"My mother was French. My father met and married her when we were at war with France on the continent."

She indicated the younger of the two children, both dressed the same in loose smocks. "This is Aimée and here is Simon."

"And your name?"

"Gabrielle Guillet. Call me Gaby." She scattered hand-carved wooden blocks of the alphabet on the floor for the children. "They were made by a prisoner from France. He'd been conscripted into the army. He taught us how to read."

"There's no schooling here then?"

"There is if you can afford it. Some of the wealthy have tutors for their children."

A role his father could play! If he could find out which families!

Gaby hadn't finished. "Some, like a friend of mine, are sent to France to be educated. But her father owned several fishing vessels."

There was silence. His eyes met hers without flinching. "Now you know I'm British, will you betray me?"

"How could I? You saved my life. What would have happened to the babies if I'd gone down under the waves forever or been washed ashore up the coast?"

"But why were you out there at all? The waves were enormous! The fog as thick as a woollen blanket! And there's a battle on! What made you do it?"

"Hunger. I needed food for the babies, so I went to cast a net while the town slept, and others were praying in the chapel."

"I heard the chanting."

"It goes on all day long. There's a reason. Our town supplies are almost gone." Her eyes filled with tears, she looked down at the babies. "Only the Holy Mother can keep them from starving."

"But what about the rest of your family?"

"Last September there was a terrible gale. A British ship foundered beyond the harbour mouth."

A British ship! He felt a sudden sickness in the pit of his stomach. *His father!*

Unaware of his anxiety, she went on. "My father went out to try to rescue some of the sailors."

"From a British ship?"

"Yes, but the real battle hadn't begun then. They were human beings just like him, in danger on the sea. He drowned with them."

His alarm grew, even as he longed to put a hand out to her. "Were there many British ships wrecked?"

"Many. Some lost their masts, others were driven on to the rocks and torn apart. Some of our schooners right here on the shore were smashed." She sounded bewildered. "The sea was so ferocious it reached a little lake two leagues inland!"

Philippe looked down. His hands trembled. "Were many British washed ashore?"

"None alive. We held a special mass for them and our own. They were all victims of the fierce Atlantic. And now we're all victims of war."

Philippe tried to keep calm. *His father had set out long before September — surely he'd have been put safely ashore in some secret harbour before the gale.* "And your father gave his life for British sailors."

"Yes, and he and his boat were never seen again. But then you were there to rescue me!"

"Your mother?"

"Several months ago some sailors from a trading ship brought the pox ashore and many of our town people died of it, my mother among them." Once again, Gaby's eyes filled with tears. "Does that make you afraid?"

"Of course not. Why?"

"Many think they see the disease lurking in all the corners. That's why you're safe here. Nosey folks like Monsieur Dutot will venture in but not for long."

She saw him glance down at the clothes she'd given him. "My older brother's. He ran away to join a privateer."

"A pirate ship!"

"Oh yes! There are plenty of them out there — old soldiers and sailors no use to anybody when peace came, or just plain deserters looking for riches on the high seas."

"And your brother ran away to join them?"

"It was an adventure, far more exciting than catching cod."

"Do you ever hear of him?"

"Never." Again her eyes brimmed with tears. "The British ship they challenged boarded and sank them. Like my father, he was drowned. Can you wonder I'll do anything to save the babies?"

He took her hand in his own and held it tightly. "You have me now, I'll help you."

She didn't take her hand away. "Can you tell me why you're here? Why you were hiding? You speak French like one of us."

"I was lucky. I told you I had an English father and a French mother."

"Had?"

With heavy rains pounding the roof and a rising wind rattling the windows they stayed close to the fire as Philippe shared his story. Without dwelling on any detail that might disclose his father's true mission, he told how, eight months previously, they'd seen his father board a British ship and had heard nothing since. "My mother died of a quick fever shortly after he left. The young ones were sent to our grandparents in France. To share the terrible news, I had to come to search for my father, all the way from Acadia, where we'd been stationed with him. We heard rumours that the ship was headed for Isle Royale," he paused, "and that's why I'm here." Now more than ever, he thought, with a foot in both camps.

She went to make up the fire. "Acadia where the British began to drive the French from their homes three years ago, and go on doing so." There was restrained anger in her voice.

How could he explain the ugliness of that event? Even his father had railed against it, perhaps because of his mother's French blood. "Acadia was given to the British by treaty. They were afraid the French settlers there would betray them from within. My mother was spared, of course, because she was the wife of a British officer."

All the sadness of her life was in Gaby's cry. "Wars! Why do men fight them?"

"For greed and power. Your Fortress Louisbourg is a danger to the British in New England, and wherever they're settled in this new land. That's why the British fleet is out there in the bay." He tried not to think of divided loyalties. "But I promise to help you and the babies, until I find my father." *And oh, how he wished he could be sure of that!*

"You think he could have swum ashore here then, from a wrecked British ship? You believe he's still alive?"

"I'm sure of it." He didn't tell her it was a spy's business to stay alive and he wouldn't have swum ashore. He'd have been put ashore in a remote spot, somewhere far safer. And he, Philippe, would have to discover what disguise his father had assumed in the fortress and tell him of his wife's death.

Night had fallen when Philippe's story was ended. Rain and wind still mingled with sounds of battle. A great shout came at the door. Gaby ran to open it. On the threshold was the biggest man Philippe had ever seen. He towered above them like a giant. His face was round and strangely innocent, like a child's. Astonished, he eyed Philippe. Gaby faced him directly. Some unspoken message passed between them. "My cousin, Philippe, come from France to help me, Gros Raymond."

There were no questions. Gros Raymond spoke. "Philippe, I need your help. A woman in the next street has been struck by shell fragments. Help me get her into the house so I can stem the bleeding."

In a flash, Philippe was after him. In the damaged house, confusion reigned. A young man cradled a woman, perhaps his wife, in his arms. Gros Raymond took charge. "Andre, this is Philippe, Gaby's cousin. We'll take her to Gaby's house first. The three of us will lift her to lessen the danger of bleeding. Careful now."

As tenderly as if she were a baby, the huge man lifted the woman, directing the others where to place their arms. Gaby was waiting at her door. "I've torn up some old skirts to bind her with. Will you take her to the hospital, Gros Raymond?"

"Oui, when I know she won't bleed to death."

He'd done this before, Philippe could see that. With sure, deft fingers, Gros Raymond bound the wounds and stopped the bleeding.

"I'll go with you to carry her to the hospital," Philippe offered. What a chance to see if his father was among hospital helpers or patients!

"Well and good, boy. André, you go to your little ones. We'll look after her. Philippe, lift her legs carefully. Follow!"

They went down a long, dark street, the cobbles pitted with shelling. The smell of wood smoke mingled with the smell of gunfire in the damp heat of the June night.

Everywhere was confusion, sounds of weeping, shutters being opened and slammed shut again, shouts of anger or despair at the damage a shell had caused.

"It doesn't look good for the fortress, Monsieur," Philippe said quietly.

"No, Philippe, Governor Drucour and his brave wife came four years ago, determined to save us but he needs a miracle."

The massive hospital, surrounded by a thick, tall wall, loomed in the dark, an elegant spire atop it, like a beacon to the wounded. They entered an arched gateway and passed a cell with barred windows where a man sat moaning, hands and feet tied. "Poor soul," Gros Raymond muttered. "They say he's a madman. I think it likely he just wanted to escape the battle and go home to his outport."

Lanterns flickered beyond them at a door in the surrounding wall. They were met by a Brother of Charity, one of those who ran the hospital. He made the sign of the cross and addressed Gros Raymond. "Is she dying?"

"No, praise God, only badly wounded."

"We'll tend to the wounds as best we can and then you must get her home. We can't take many more. We're overcrowded with wounded soldiers, sailors with fevers from the ships, many a sick citizen. Get the boy to help you carry her to a pallet." Then he was gone.

They found a straw mattress to lay her on and Gros Raymond turned to Philippe. "I have other duties to tend to here, boy. You'd best get home to Gabrielle and the babies and see what you can do for them."

"Yes, Monsieur." But Philippe had no intention of leaving. He had to discover if his father was here. The foul smell of illness and death, of feces and urine was all around him. It almost suffocated him, but he had to linger to cast a quick glance at every bed in the ward. Most of the patients were soldiers, lying on their backs, their faces masks of agony, their moans an ongoing refrain. Others appeared to be in a deep coma. Philippe wondered if some of them would ever wake again. There were so few helpers, and even fewer Brothers of Charity. When he saw a soldier, weak and wounded, being helped to the latrine, he sprang forward to give an arm, his presence, as a friend of Gros Raymond's, unquestioned. He saw a soldier being bled to reduce his fever. The cries and groans seemed to grow louder until he could hardly bear it but he knew he must. His father, in whatever guise, must be found. He went on, peering into the three other wards, marvelling at the friars' ability to manage at all with the beds filled and patients lying on the floor between them. He continued to help where he could, carrying buckets, assisting in turning a wounded body, and even rushing with a mop to clean up vomit from the floor. They accepted him as one of themselves. Oddly enough, he felt that he was.

He wandered on, finding the chapel where several wounded men, tightly bandaged, were on their knees, praying. In a nearby cubicle, an apothecary bade him pound some herbs with a pestle. Even that small workplace was invaded with the odour of unwashed bodies. The laundry was worse, soiled and blood-soaked bandages piled in heaps and the sweating attendant hardly able to cope.

When he reached the kitchen and the bakery, he felt some relief from the need to be sick. The aromas here were of soup and bread, fresh from the oven. He suddenly had a pot of stew and a huge loaf of bread shoved at him and was told which ward to take it to. "And here's a loaf for yourself, lad. You may need that later to keep going."

He accepted with a heart full of thanks. Something to take home to Gaby and the children. He hid the loaf in his shirt, and delivered the food to the ward servant, cringing as a huge rat ran across his path and roaches crawled from a corner. Sadly, he gave up his search. Yet he rejoiced in the gift he was bringing.

The Mysterious Monk

It was on his way to Gaby's that he saw the white figure again, holding a sick child tenderly in his arms. *Who was he?* He'd known religious orders who wore white robes, the Cistercians for one. They had an abbey, his mother had told him, near her birthplace in France. But he'd never heard of them here in the New World. He knew the Récollet friars looked after spiritual affairs in the fortress and he'd seen the Brothers of Charity at work in the hospital but neither order wore white.

Who could this stranger be, first of all gliding along in the dark like the ghost Philippe first took him to be and then here, bearing a sick child like a loving nurse? Gaby might know. He must hasten home to ask.

By the time he reached her street the fog had thickened. He peered through the darkness trying to locate the house. He knew he must beware of Monsieur Dutot. Even if everyone else accepted him without question, the cobbler's suspicions could be easily aroused at Philippe's constant presence in Gaby's home. But suddenly, almost at Gaby's door, there he was, face to face with her neighbour. The other backed off and glared at him. "Who are you?"

Philippe caught sight of Jonas behind the cobbler, tugging a load of firewood. "Good evening, Monsieur," he said. "I'm Gaby's cousin from France." He hoped the cobbler wouldn't hear his heart pounding.

"From France, eh?"

"Yes, Monsieur, from Normandy. I thought I'd try life in the New World, but I've come at a bad time."

Even in the dim light, Philippe could see disbelief on the cobbler's face. "When did you come? How could you get here with the harbour blockaded?"

"Oh, I came before the British, Monsieur. I've been foraging for food in the countryside." At least that much was true. God forgive him the other lies!

Monsieur Dutot spat into the street. "The blasted British! We'll hang every last man of them! Did you hear they tried to make a landing today?"

"What happened?"

"Word has it that they set out in the small boats early this morning to find a way to shore, but they had to retreat. For once this everlasting fog did us some good." He turned unexpectedly and gave Jonas a great clout on the head. "Why are you standing there staring, oaf! Get your load home and set about your other duties!"

Philippe winced at the pain on the slave's face. He watched him move away, the load obviously too large for his small frame. "Let's hope the British have as little success every day, Monsieur. Our defences are strong. Again, good night to you, Monsieur!" He moved quickly, conscious of the cobbler's eyes following him to Gaby's door.

He was inside in a moment, sharing news of the hospital, Monsieur Dutot and the failed landing attempt. With a flourish he produced the bread he'd been given. He took Aimée on his knee. "Gaby, who's the ghost who wanders your streets so silently?"

"Ghost? I don't know of such a thing! There may be a few after these days of shelling!"

"It's a figure in a monk's robe. I've seen him several times, slipping along through the dark as if he had wings."

"There are the Recollet friars who tend the affairs of the spirit in the fortress and the hospital, even aboard the ships."

"But they wear brown habits. This one was all in white."

Gaby smiled warmly. "Ah, you mean the Monk!"

"Hasn't he a name?"

"None. He doesn't speak. He just appeared among us one day last year."

A sudden thought made Philippe's hopes rise. *It could be his father! It could be!* He tried to sound calm. "Where did he come from?"

"No one seems to know. The story goes that he was disfigured in a fire or in battle. Perhaps in the siege of '45."

"And that's why he covers his face and neck with the cowl?"

"That's what they say, to hide the scars."

What a perfect disguise for his father. It must be he! "What does he do?"

"Only good. He brings food to us whenever he can. He's helped nurse the sick and tend the wounded ever since the siege began."

"And nobody at all knows who he is?"

"Nobody. But we don't care. He's been so good to all of us, especially the helpless and lonely."

Philippe was filled with pride. *What a disguise his father had chosen — no one would question the comings and goings of a hardworking monk! He could speak to anyone, gather information anywhere. But how would he be getting it to the British?* Another thought struck Philippe. The enemy his father was spying on was Gaby, her neighbours and friends, not just nameless soldiers in a barracks.

"Is something wrong?" Gaby was staring at his troubled face. "Are you tired? Would you like to sleep?"

"Oh, no! No!" A change of subject would be safe. "How did your father come to Louisbourg, Gaby?"

"It was my grandparents who came from France to find a new life. The British attacked and took over the town in '45. My grandfather was killed but my grandmother refused to be sent back to Brittany with the others. She fled to the forest with her son, my father, his wife, my mother and their new-born, me. The Micmacs helped us survive."

"Did she return then, four years later, when France was given back the fortress?"

"She did and somehow she managed to buy a rowboat to start a fishing business." Gaby looked proud. "It grew and grew. My grandmother was a wonderfully brave woman."

"Your father inherited the business then?"

"Yes, and he managed to buy a chaloupe and hired two men to help him. When he drowned his helpers gave me a dory. Now that's gone too," she hung her head, "because of my stupidity."

"We'll have to start a new life then, like your grandmother." For her sake, Philippe said it with a cheer he didn't feel. He laid the sleeping Aimée on the bed. "Somehow we'll manage together. As soon as possible, I'll go down to the quay to search for news." *And for the Monk who could be his father.*

"You won't find it like the old days before the siege began," Gaby said. "Then there'd be fishermen haggling over the price of fish as they unloaded their vessels at the dock, and all kinds of trading ships."

"It'll be a war zone now," Philippe said.

His fitful sleep that night was punctuated by the sharp whine of shells the French were lobbing into the British ships in the bay and the answering retorts. Eventually weariness overcame him and he fell deeply asleep.

A huge explosion of gunfire wakened him in the night. That made up his mind. A trip to the quay might be wiser when the barrage had lessened. More citizens would venture there in greater safety and his presence would not be noticed or questioned. Content with his decision, again he slept.

A Runaway in the Dark

The days following found him on the back streets making
himself familiar to the town citizens, but still searching. When
the loved, familiar face failed to appear, he found satisfaction
in bringing Gaby small offerings of food left scattered by
explosions or the retreat of homeowners to safer quarters. A
small bowl of lard here, a measure of peas there, a bag of
corn abandoned, all were welcomed with delight. His own
findings were enriched by those from Jonas, who left a large
square of blanket, a patched cloak and once a whole ham-
bone, meat still clinging, a little rancid but perfect for the stew-
pot at the hearth. One night, hearing Jonas at the door,
Philippe opened it as the slave deposited his gift. It was then
he caught a swift glimpse of the welts and scars on the boy's
hands and arms, painful evidence of his master's cruelty.

If Philippe or Gaby wondered about the source of the
bounty, they said nothing, not even when the gifts were a pair
of leather shoes, almost new — a perfect fit for Gaby, alongside two whole loaves of wheaten bread. In a time of war, sur-
vival brooked no doubts or questions.

One morning, he awoke to silence and darkness. The
guns had ceased firing and a light fog cloaked the town.

Gaby was aware of it first. "It's a morning for the quay," she
said. "The fog has stopped the attack for now. There'll be

more people down there looking for news and the fog isn't so thick that you can't search among them, if you really believe your father could have come to the fortress."

"Perhaps even to one of the outports after the shipwrecks in that gale," Philippe suggested. But he was silent about his father's true intentions, hoping she wouldn't ask why his father wouldn't have tried to rejoin the British fleet. In her innocent trust, she did not.

"Go quickly," she warned. "The fog may burn off and the barrage will begin again. It won't be safe for you or anybody down there then."

He hastened to wash and dress. After giving Gaby a hand with the children, and breakfasting on dry bread and warm milk, he slipped out into the half-light, wary of the cobbler's nearness. There was no candle lit in that house. For the moment he was safe. He felt no uncertainty until he was passing a large building on his left. It appeared to be partially destroyed, perhaps by the hurricane force gales some time ago.

He heard a whisper "Help me. Come over here and help me!"

He froze. *Who could it be? Was it a trap to catch him? Had someone discovered who he really was?*

The whisper came again. "Over here. In the bushes!"

A child's voice! Hardly someone to mean him harm. He crept closer. Then he saw the face, elfin and wide-eyed. It peered at him through a clump of flowers. She was like a little flower herself, even though the long hair straggled to her shoulders untidily, and her nightshift hung too large around her shoulders. He leaned close. "Why do you need help? Who are you?"

"Shh! I'm Emilie. I'm running away!"

"Running away?" Didn't she know about the British in the bay and the shelling? "Running away from what?" He bent close to hear her answer.

"From here, of course. From the Sisters of the Congregation!"

He knew at once. "This must be the nunnery then. You live here with the Sisters?"

"Where else would I live? I'm an orphan. They look after all the orphans."

"But why do you want to leave? Where would you go?"

The child shrugged in her thin shift. "Anywhere to get away. I just learned something a week ago. I don't belong here."

Philippe heard shouts approaching on the street. Soldiers? Citizens abroad early? He didn't wait to find out. He crept into the bushes with the child, hidden as the shouting passed. He could see the nunnery garden behind them.

"Why don't you belong, Emilie?"

"Because I heard a secret. I'm not French at all. I'm English."

"How can you know that? French is your language!"

She pulled him closer. "A woman came to the nunnery last week. She'd been beaten by her husband and came for shelter. I was doing a sampler in the corner because I'd been naughty. I heard Sister Cécile tell the woman I'd been left behind by the British when the French took the fortress over nine years ago. I guess I was a baby then. Maybe they found me, like Moses, in the bulrushes."

The child was so appealing, Philippe forgot his own mission. "But the Sisters have cared for you, haven't they? They're good to you?"

"What's so good when we run out of food and firewood because there's no money to buy any more? And then there are all those lessons in reading and writing and silly old needlework. And straw mattresses to make for the soldiers!"

Philippe smiled. "Don't you do anything for fun?"

"Playing the flute sometimes or the harpsichord. But I get all the notes wrong and then I have to go back to memorizing the catechism and learning the lives of the saints. I don't want to be any saint!"

Not much chance of that, Philippe thought. "What would you rather be doing?"

"I'd like to be a fisherman or paddle in the ocean."

"Not these days you wouldn't, Emilie. Can't you hear the gunfire? There's a war on. The British are all around us." For a moment he forgot he was one himself. "Where would you run to?"

"To them, of course! Then I could find out who I really am. Why would anybody leave me, a baby, like that?" Her eyes filled with tears.

"Can't you try to be happy here for now? The Sisters will protect you as long as they can. Emilie, if you learn your lessons, how to read and write, one day you'll be free to do what you want."

"No, I won't. I'll have to go and work as a servant in one of the rich merchant's houses. I'll sleep in a little hole some-where and eat the slops from the table. Marie had to go and she was only seven!"

Philippe wondered whether she would be glad or sorry to learn that there might be very few rich merchants left.

"Marie — was she someone you cared about?"

"Oh, yes! Not as much as I like Denise, she's my special friend. The Monk, too — sometimes he comes to the garden, and brings me treats. Then there's Antoine. He's my favourite."

"And who is he?"

"The gardener and helper around the nunnery. He came here a few months ago. He even plays games with me when the Sisters aren't looking."

Philippe's hopes rose. Another possibility! "Where did he come from?"

"Somewhere in the forest. I think he'd been working on a farm near one of the outports."

Just then another whisper came, harsh with anxiety. "Emilie! Emilie, where are you?"

"I knew it! That's Antoine. Now I can't get away! Why didn't you help me?"

Antoine was there before he could answer. "Emilie, what are you doing out here again? Where do you think you can run to, little one?"

Philippe's spirits sank. This man was short and stocky, his face lined beneath a thatch of greying hair. His own father was tall, slim and handsome. Another hope gone.

Antoine had caught sight of him in the growing light. Accusingly, he glared at him, "Who are you? Were you trying to help her get away?"

"Monsieur Antoine, I could never help her get away. There's nowhere to run to! I'm Gabrielle Guillet's cousin from France, trying to help her through the siege."

"Poor lass. She's without father and mother, like this one here."

"Monsieur, what will happen to her and the nunnery when the battle grows greater?"

"I know what will happen," Antoine said fiercely. "The British are trying to gain a foothold on the beach. If they do they'll get to the hills and marshes behind the fortress and destroy us all. We're open to cannon and mortar fire on all sides then. They won't be worried about nunneries or innocents."

Gaby and the children! Philippe's alarm grew. "What will you do?"

In a sudden gesture, Antoine drew the silent Emilie to him. "I'll protect her. We'll flee to the forest. I came from there. If we can keep out of sight of the British, there's a living to be made along the coast or perhaps on the banks of the Mira River. She'll be my own child." He eyed Philippe, as if wondering how much to tell. "I lost both wife and child some years ago in a fire."

Philippe was relieved — this child would be cared for, whatever happened. Now he had to move. "Monsieur, I must be on my way to find food and any news that's to be learned on the quay. I wish you God's blessings."

"And you, young sir." Swiftly, Antoine set off behind the nunnery. "I'll get her back to her bed before they find out she's gone or there'll be more punishment. May God save us all!"

"May He, indeed!" Philippe whispered, making off down the cobbled street.

Full daylight came with a clear sky and the fog dispersed, as Gaby had predicted. It would be, after all, a perfect day for the British to storm the shore. Shaking off his knowledge of what this meant for the citizens of Louisbourg, he focused on his task. All about him, well-clad merchants, their wigs and tri-corne hats askew in their urgency, sought news from one another. They deplored the state of the small boats. These, used to reach the larger ships beyond the shallows, had been smashed by the shelling against the quay. The quay itself was, indeed, a war zone. The small inns and lodgings for sailors and the once-popular taverns were now deserted, doors and windows barricaded, their former clientele manning the barri-cades, sleeping in corners and leaning against walls to recov-er enough strength to go on with the battle. One soldier had energy enough to start up at the sight of a strong-looking lad with idle hands.

"Hey, you there!" he shouted to Philippe.

Swiftly Philippe slipped out of sight. He passed a huge wooden block no doubt used to auction slaves. Then he joined an odd procession moving in the direction of the chapel. A funeral, led by a priest bearing a cross! A small crowd followed and Philippe followed them. This must be a very important person to justify a ceremony in the midst of battle. Quickly he left the band of mourners and darted into a side street.

It was then he saw the Monk again, bending over a wounded soldier, bandaging his chest. He drew closer, needing to see if this was his father's disguise. The Monk turned quickly to face him. One bright blue eye stared at him but not unkindly. This was not his father then, his eyes were brown.

The Monk turned away to tend the wounded and sadly deflated, Philippe turned away, too. When he was at Gaby's door again, she drew him in quickly. "Monsieur of the long nose has been here again," she said. "He suspects something."

"Monsieur Dutot?"

"One and the same. What of you? What did you find out?"

Quietly, devouring peas and bread, he told her of his ventures. When he spoke of Emilie, he said, "Would they really send her out as a servant?"

"More than likely. Where else would she go? She'd empty the slops, wash the clothes in the brook outside the town gate, sweep floors, wash dishes, even feed the chickens and probably sleep with them on rags in the henhouse!"

"Well, there may be a worse fate in store for her than even that, for all of the fortress. The British are about to land on the beach." He detailed for her what he had heard.

Tears began to stream down Gaby's face. "What is to become of our babies?" She looked in despair where they played on the floor with a hand-carved ball. "Shall we all die?"

For a moment he was silent, suddenly seeing Gaby as if for the first time. The slim upright figure, attractive even in cast-off damask, the lovely oval face framed by an abundance of shining black hair, the sad anxious eyes, forever gazing down at her little ones, wondering what sacrifices she could make to keep them alive. Somehow she had crept into his heart and he knew she would stay there.

He was aware that she had repeated her question. "Philippe, are we all to die? Please! What are we to do?"

"We'll get away from the fortress, as faraway as possible and find a new life." A new life he knew it had to be. Gone were all doubts as to where his loyalties lay. He would abandon his search for his father and give all his mind and heart to saving Gaby and the babies, his new family.

"How can we?"

"With help from your friends. We'll find a way through holes in the wall and the palisade made by the British guns. We'll cross the marshes to the forest, and then we'll head for a farm where I sheltered on my way here, Luc Gabon's. We'll be safer there."

Sudden hope shone in her eyes. "Is it possible, Philippe? Really possible?"

"It is but we'll have to plan every move with caution."

Alarm flared on her face. "What about Jonas? After all he has done for us, I can't leave him to be knocked about by his new captors."

"We'll take him with us." Philippe's decision was immediate. "He'll be one more to help with the babies."

"If we're found stealing a slave there'll be terrible penalties to pay. And Jonas will suffer the most for running away."

"Then we mustn't be found. We'll be ever on the watch. I've seen you praying by your bed. Pray to Jesus and the Blessed Virgin now, for their protection."

"I shall, I shall!" She fell on her knees at once and Philippe saw her lips moving in an urgency of prayer. She started up at a drumming on the door.

"Monsieur Dutot again," she whispered. "Be calm." But Philippe heard the relief in her voice. "Oh, Gros Raymond. Come in! I'm so glad it's you."

Gros Raymond's huge figure filled the room. He saw the tears on her face. "What's the matter, girl? Is there something I can do for you?"

Philippe cut in. "Gros Raymond, I heard that if the British land on the beaches, they'll push their cannon up behind the town into the marshes. No one will be safe then. I want to get Gaby and the babies away."

Gros Raymond clasped him round the shoulders. "Good lad. It's a wise plan, and I'll help you. But can you help me first?"

"Anything I can do, Gros Raymond, I will."

"Women and children are sheltering in one of the casemates, the rooms inside the fortress walls. I need to take food and medicine there."

"I'm with you." At once, Philippe followed him out the door, watched him heave a huge sack of goods to his shoulder and accepted two smaller but still heavy bags for his own.

The desolation of the shelling was everywhere. Weeping came to them over the sound of gunfire. A voice screamed, "Help me! Help me!" then fell silent. A brown-robed Récollet friar passed them, his wooden clogs covering bare feet, clattering over the cobbles. "On his way to give last rites to the dying, no doubt," Gros Raymond said. "They need a little comfort themselves, those friars. Miserably housed, poorly fed, and even providing their own beds."

"A Récollet friar shared a meal with me when I was on the trail here. He'd been to an outpost to give last rites there, too!" Suddenly he realized what he'd confessed, that he had come by land and not by sea from France! He held his breath.

Gros Raymond smiled at him, quickly, knowingly but said only, "Here are the casemates, lad. Be prepared for unhappy scenes."

The vaulted cavern they entered was filled with the moans of the sick and the cries of children. The stench of urine, illness and death was all around them. "Here, follow me, while I give comfort where I can." Gros Raymond pointed to a makeshift shelter of blankets at the far end. Philippe heard cries of agony. "A baby coming into the world with the help of the Widow Droit. Wait here. I'll take some easing drugs with me." He was back in a moment. A lusty wail filled the cavern. Gros Raymond's smile was sad. "A fine boy, born into war. God send him safely to France, if the British win this one."

They worked together feverishly, tending to sickness, administering opiates, apportioning food. When they were finished, Philippe was glad to step into the open air even if it was racked by shellfire. He decided to be honest with this selfless man. "Gros Raymond, we want to take Jonas with us. Can you help?"

"I can get a message to him. I talk to all and sundry in town so no one can suspect me of anything but good. And good is what you and I want for Jonas."

"Tell him to meet me in the warehouse on the Rue de Quay at ten tonight, the one by the blue tavern. Most good citizens should be in their beds by then."

"For my part I'll pay a friendly call on Monsieur Dutot at nine-thirty to discuss the state of the battle. I'll keep him arguing until well after eleven. Can you get away before then?"

"If Jonas comes with us at once."

Gros Raymond's face mirrored concern. "Lad, where are you going to head for?"

Philippe drew a deep breath. Now this man would know all.

"Monsieur, on the way here I hid in the marsh hay on the other side of Gabarus Bay. Luc Gabon, a farmer, found me there."

"Farms are rare around here. Too much rock and swamp."

"It wasn't much of a farm, a few animals and a small patch of garden. His wife was expecting a child, so I was able to be of help to them, even in the cabin."

"They'll take you all in, no doubt of that." He gripped Philippe's shoulder. "You do realize you'll be punished if you're caught with the slave boy?"

"Gros Raymond, Jonas saved my life. I must save his. Will you help?"

Gros Raymond took the two empty sacks from Philippe. "I'll fill these with food, candles, a horn candle holder, flints and a flagon for water, too. And leave them after dark between this house and Dutot's. In the larger sack I'll put the sketch of a way to get safely to the marshes. From there on, you're on your own."

Philippe's eyes filled with tears. "God keep you, Gros Raymond!"

"And you, lad, and all of us." Then they were at Gaby's door and Gros Raymond was gone.

Flight to the Forest

Nightfall seemed forever coming. He planned with Gabrielle what to take and told her of the sacks Gros Raymond was leaving. They gathered meagre possessions into some kind of manageable load, tearing up threadbare sheets to make back-packs for carrying the children. They rolled blankets into a bundle, the little ones' clogs tucked inside.

"Philippe, I'm worried about food."

"We'll take what we have from here, along with Gros Raymond's offering, then we'll find roots and berries and last year's nuts. That's what I did on my way here."

At last it was dark enough for him to venture forth. He glanced quickly at Monsieur Dutot's house. Light streamed from beneath the door. Voices rose and fell inside. Gros Raymond had kept his promise. There, hidden between the houses, were the two bulging sacks he'd prepared.

Silently but swiftly — he knew the town well, now — he made his way through the shadowy streets. The houses were shuttered and quiet, inns and taverns silent, too, doors and windows barricaded. The warehouse next to the blue tavern had one door swinging wide, the other held closed by coils of rope. He slipped in the open door. The sweet smell of molasses from the West Indies filled his nostrils. He ducked behind the barrels to watch and listen for Jonas, glad of his concealment, when he heard he was not alone. *Where were the voices coming from?* Peering out from his hiding place, he saw two figures huddled in a corner crowded with sailing gear.

"We're bound to win, my love. How can you doubt it?" A soldier and his girl! Probably a servant from one of the merchant's houses, under cover of night, taking a last chance to meet her lover.

He heard her sobbing. "How can we win? So many ships, so many soldiers out there in the harbour! Already their guns have destroyed most of our town! They'll win and kill us all!"

"Don't you believe it. Today while we were on sentry duty we heard that Madame Drucour, the governor's wife is going to the ramparts! Our captain said she'll fire on the enemy herself. That'll put some heart into the troops. She's a brave woman, that one!"

Philippe couldn't hear the girl's reply. They moved off, towards the open door, so close he could have touched them. *But where was Jonas?* He knew Gros Raymond would have delivered the message.

The whispered answer came. "Massa! Massa! Here!"

Here? Where was here? Bewildered, he peered around. No shadow showed. No face was hidden among barrels or coils of rope.

"Up, Massa! Look up!"

He did. Frightened eyes stared at him over a swatch of rolled sailcloth suspended from the rafters. His whisper was hoarse. "Jonas, come down now! We have to leave!"

"Massa, I fearing! What to do? What to do?"

"You'll be safe with us. We'll protect you from now on. But come! We can't waste time! I promise we'll look after you!" With God's help and a lot of luck, he added to himself.

His body shaking, the boy slithered down the ropes. Philippe put an arm around the thin shoulders. "We have to get Gaby and the babies now. Just do as I say."

Suddenly, more noise! They crouched, waiting. Three soldiers staggered in wearily to roll more barrels out to the quay. When their steps had faded into the clamour of guns, Philippe and Jonas slipped like shadows out of the warehouse and back to Gaby's street. Philippe had just noted the candlelight streaming from Dutot's house when his door crashed open. With a movement like lightning, Philippe yanked Jonas to the recess between two houses.

Raging, Monsieur Dutot, barged into the street. "Where is he? He was supposed to be back an hour ago with more firewood!"

"We have plenty to go on." Gros Raymond's voice was soft, cajoling. "He's probably looking for more food for you, too."

"Wait till I lay my hands on him! He'll know when to come back the next time. A triple lashing is too good for him!"

Philippe felt Jonas tremble beside him.

"Monsieur Dutot, calm yourself. Come inside. You'll need all your strength for what we have to face in the days to come." Gently Gros Raymond drew him in. The door closed.

Gaby was waiting for them, the two little ones wrapped and sleeping in backpacks. "I brought in the sacks and gave the babies a sleeping draught of herbs Gros Raymond put there for them. And here's the map he promised." She mouthed the words.

It was a simple one and Philippe memorized it quickly. "It's when we get out on the streets we need to whisper, Gaby. Have you the food and the tinder box in the other sacks?"

"Everything we need." She eyed Philippe, troubled. "Philippe, are we doing the right thing?"

"The only thing to keep you and the babies alive."

"But Jonas? I know we want to take Jonas, Philippe. But I worry about breaking the law."

"We can't go without him when we know what he did for both of us. Slave or free, he deserves a life, Gaby, and we owe him that."

"If they find us?"

"We'll have to hide him. Now come, we've no time to waste. Leave the candle to gutter out and follow me. Keep close to the walls. Understand, Jonas?"

"Yes, Massa."

Philippe went out first. The street was empty. He beckoned to the others. With an anguished backwards glance at her home, Gaby silently closed the door. They were on their way, gunfire from the shore echoing in the distance.

The weather befriended them. A light fog muffled their movement along the deserted cobbled back lanes of the fortress. Philippe followed Gros Raymond's map, unerringly. Only once was there a moment of real fear. A door swung open to the night around them. Three men erupted into the street in an explosion of argument and swearing. Like ghosts Philippe and the others melted into a nearby wood lot, still as statues. Then the men were gone. Again they crept along the shelled section of the fortress wall indicated by Gros Raymond's map.

Philippe whispered, "A sentry's patrolling the ramparts. When he moves east, we move forward. Can you see any way out down there in the ruins of the wall?"

The other two nodded, silent, pointing.

Philippe saw it, too. Gros Raymond had plotted their course well. "It'll be a tight squeeze with the babies. Jonas, when we start, you go through first and take them one at a time. Keep close to the wall on the other side. We'll follow at once."

"Yes, Massa."

Like a hawk his prey, Philippe watched the sentry. "Now!" They moved like a small disciplined army towards the broken wall, pushing Jonas, then the babies through. The wall had been immensely thick and the towering heaps of mortar and stones made the opening almost impassable. But slowly, carefully, Jonas scrabbled over broken masonry with Aimée. Then, his face shining with success, he came back for Simon. Gaby clawed her way through, followed by Philippe. It seemed to take forever. They heard the sentry's boots ringing on the fortress wall close by as they made it to the other side and crouched together, hidden, until again he moved on. At last they were all beyond the rubble, gathering up the sleeping babies.

"This part is tricky," Philippe warned. "There's water in the ditch from the rains but we'll have to keep as close to the ground as possible. I'll go first to give you a hand down."

They heard the clomp, clomp, of the sentry's advance and hugged the ground. With that sound fading they began again, slithering down to the ditch, then inch-by-inch, seeking toe-holds in the low stonewall atop another rise. The fog was their friend. The farther they moved from the main fortress wall, the less likely it was they could be seen.

The palisade was still to come.

"Along here there's a place where the British guns have shattered the palings," Philippe whispered. "Can you see it?"

They all lay, like cornered mice, staring into the night. *Dear God!* From Philippe it was a prayer. *Were they to fail because they couldn't see a few broken sticks?*

"Massa, look!" Jonas pointed to the west.

There it was, a large gap in the wooden stockade and not too faraway! God keep Jonas! He'd saved them again!

"Wait for the sentry!" Philippe warned. Then once more they were moving, squirming between broken stakes, tearing their clothes in their haste.

"God be thanked!" Philippe breathed. "We're through!" On her knees, Gaby murmured prayers. Philippe touched her shoulder. "We'll thank God as we go. We still have the huge mound of the glacis to cover. Remember, this is where the sentries have advance sight of an attack from the rear. Hug the ground! The fog will help us!"

The babies on their backs, they plunged forward, hearts pounding, expecting a shout from the fortress wall. None came.

But the ground ahead was waiting to entrap them. If the first part of the escape had seemed difficult, it was nothing compared to the next. All the terrain they had to cover between the glacis and the welcoming trees was a mass of bogs, hillocks and marsh. They slithered and crawled in and out of water, through tightly tangled marsh bracken, up and down slimy slopes. The babies were heavy on their backs, Jonas behind them.

Hours later they staggered, almost sobbing with relief, into the shelter of the trees. Without speaking, they all collapsed on the ground. Then Gaby knelt, thanking God. Even as she knelt, they saw a great fire explode in the sky where a British shell had landed. The walls of the once-proud fortress, looked, in its glare, like the crumbling defences of a mighty castle going down to defeat.

A Body in the Water

"Gaby! Jonas! We can't stop here. It's too close to the fortress!" Philippe shook them awake in the darkness. "We'll rest later. It'll be safer."

Staggering with sleep and exhaustion, they made their way deeper into the forest. An ancient woodcutter's trail made the going easier. Old trees, twisted into witchy shapes by Atlantic gales, loomed beside them. Then, an hour later, they came on a bosky dell of spruce and birch.

"This is the place," Philippe decided. "We'll pull down some spruce boughs to lie on, and cover ourselves with the old blankets we've brought."

Gaby said, "Aren't we still too close? In the last siege, some of our people fled to the forest to hide their valuables and the British found them and shot them."

"They won't find us. They're too busy with the bombardment. Let's huddle together now and keep the babies warm between us." That done, they slept.

"Massa! Massa, wake up!" Jonas was shaking him and calling in English. "Massa, there's a screaming! Wake up!"

Philippe forced his eyes open. The dawn was coming. Even in the darkness of the dell, the screaming was loud.

"What is it?" Gaby sat up, her eyes round with fear.

Philippe listened. "Gulls! The gulls have been disturbed

on the shore!" He tried to shake himself awake. "I'm going there to find out what's happening."

"No, no, Massa. Don't go! I fearing!"

"I must, Jonas. I want to know what's going on so I can make plans for us. You watch over Gaby and the babies."

He trod softly through the forest, the sounds of the ocean pounding on the shore, and the shelling, growing closer with every step. He knew that hundreds of French soldiers were hidden along the shores and cliffs. But he'd take his chances and hope to evade them or manufacture some excuse if they saw him.

He squirmed along the ground until he came to the edge of the forest, and the cliffs. He heard the French guns firing on his left and realized he and his little family had travelled beyond the main battle. Still, he felt almost overcome by the explosion of light and sound, the scream of shells, the boom of cannon fire.

He looked down. Drying racks for cod were still there, deserted by their owners. A chance perhaps to find some fish left there to feed Gaby and the children? What if there were a way to the beach?

He crept along the cliff edge in the half dark. There it was! A crumbling jut of land that would hide him! He squirmed down the cliff, feet first, his body flat against the land. The fish drying racks were only a few feet away. He crawled towards them. There were no dried fish there, not even a scrap. Little wonder. With the fortress starving, there'd be no scraps left anywhere. Then he saw the flash of scarlet among the boulders at the beach edge. He froze, his heart thumping. A

British soldier waiting to take a shot at him? There was no movement. He crept closer. So that was it. This soldier would never again engage in battle. He lay face down, his body caught between the rocks, staining the water with his blood. Was he dead? Could it be his father? Carefully he turned the body over. The soldier was young, not much older than his own sixteen years, and certainly dead. Sick at heart, he closed the sightless eyes. Not his father, thank God, but somebody's perhaps.

Then he realized that this soldier might have help for him. He knew he would carry, as did all British invaders, a water-proof bag of rations for sorties ashore. He found it attached to the belt, filled with bread and cheese, enough to feed them all for several meals. He knelt, said a swift prayer for the young soldier, then crawled, ration bag in hand, to the cliff. He had just gained the security of the trees when a great shout, a com-motion of voices and commands was carried on the wind amid the gunfire. Straining to see through the dawn darkness, in the far distance he discovered why. Three small British boats had somehow made it unscathed to shore, between two outcrops of rocks, safe from the French guns. Their command-er in his scarlet tunic was wading through the water, shouting triumphantly to his men to follow while the bodies of dying soldiers floated around them, the water red with their blood and the scarlet of their tunics. Musket balls whistled across the beach. They did not halt the advance. The whole cove was aflame with gun and rifle fire.

This was the end of Louisbourg then. The British had their foothold on the beach, now, and once it was secure, they would be able to launch their attack from the marshes behind the fortress, where there were few defences. He must get Jonas, Gaby and the children as faraway as possible. With one last glance at the British soldiers leaping from their boats, brandishing swords, at the wounded crawling to the shores to die there, he scrambled to safety. Suddenly a wall of flame rose above the smoke and fog. The King's Bastion! The King's Bastion had been hit! And the barracks!

Stumbling over twisted roots in haste, he fled into the forest. He clambered through clumps of spruce and larch, and an area of bog that soaked him to the skin. He found another rise of ground and for the moment felt safe. It was strange how all thoughts of his father had faded to a faint sense of loss, almost erased by his need to protect his new family. Even the English language became a thing of the past, except for Jonas's frequent use of it. They were all French together now and his mother in Heaven would be happy. While his thoughts wandered, his feet did not. He found the trail that took him back to his family and the dell. Seeing a white shape before him, he paused. Had the Monk come to seek them out? No! It was a clump of white birches, close to their camping place. He came upon Gaby and Jonas in a moment, searching for him through the trees.

"Oh, Philippe!" Gaby stretched out her arms to him. "We were so frightened you wouldn't come back!"

"Massa, I fearing! I fearing!" Jonas fell on his knees at Philippe's feet.

"No time for talk now. I'll tell you all later. We must be on our way. Has everyone been fed?"

Gaby nodded. "The babies, too, still half asleep."

"Good. I'll chew on some bread and cheese as we travel."
Philippe helped to gather up their meagre belongings, made
sure all evidence of their presence was erased and with
Aimée on his back, led the way. "Tread carefully! The snap-
ping of a broken branch could bring a soldier!" Small shrubs
and moss didn't deter their going; the trees flung down by sea
gales did. But their progress was steady, the forest more and
more like a cloak around them.

They stopped once for bread and water from the flagon,
then kept on in silence until Philippe, glancing back, saw
exhaustion on Gaby's face. "We'll stop for the night at the next
small clearing." They came upon it soon, protected by inter-
woven alder and balsam trees. Tearing balsam branches for
the ground cover, they laid the babies on them and, exhausted, flung themselves down to rest. "It's too close yet to build a
fire," Philippe decided. "We'll have to eat the cold food and
keep ourselves warm as best we can."

Like the night before, this one was spent, after prayers and
a small meal, huddled together under the thin blankets, only
the babies warm enough in their sacks. Fatigue soon overcame them, and they slept.

In the morning, Philippe took both Gaby's hands in his.
He told her what he had seen on the beach. "Gaby, with the
British ashore, Louisbourg will fall."

Gaby's eyes filled with tears, "That's the end of home then.
We can never go back."

"No, but we can go on and find a new way. Don't grieve.
It'll be a good way." Philippe bent down to pick up the still

sleeping Simon. "Let's wake the babies. We'll have food then give them more of the herbs for sleep. We must be on our way to Luc Gabon's."

They made their difficult way through the forest, the sound of battle behind them swelling and receding on the wind from the sea. They stopped beside a stream, to eat meagrely from the sacks, and fill the flagon with fresh spring water.

"Massa! A noise I hearing!" Alert for the menacing presence of his old master, it was always Jonas who heard sounds first.

Philippe stood up, quite still. "I hear nothing."

"Listen again!" Jonas pointed in the direction they'd come from.

The sounds were soft and intermittent but they were there, steps creeping in the forest behind them. Philippe motioned them to stillness, moved away from the stream and stealthily approached the thicket of trees at the top of the slope. Smiling, he returned to the others. "An animal! A lynx! He won't hurt us. There'll be more animals as we go along but it's soldiers we have to watch for."

Philippe was right. A red fox crossed their path in the early afternoon, and a white-tailed deer, shortly after, fled at their approach. They were somehow comforted to know they were not alone. Even the streams they passed or waded through were homes to marten and playful otters sliding down the banks.

Beside one of them, Gaby asked wistfully,"Can't we rest here for a while and watch them? Aren't we far enough away?"

"We'll never be that," Philippe said, "until we reach Luc Gabon's. But this is a good resting place. We'll eat and drink again and fill our flagon. We can bathe our faces, too, to refresh ourselves." He wondered if they were becoming too sure of their safety. After all, they were not that far from the fortress. Anyone could be out here waiting to challenge them, to take Jonas back to Monsieur Dutot. But he said nothing, enjoying the antics of the otters as much as the others. The delight on Jonas's face was worth taking the chance.

The little ones woke long enough to enjoy the animals' fun but, after food and drink, to Gaby's relief, quickly slept again. "At least they can't fret and be frightened at what's happening," she said. "Gros Raymond was such a friend. He'd know what to give them without harming them." And then she realized she would never see him again and turned her face away to hide her tears.

"He was," Philippe said cheerfully, "and he'd want us to keep moving and find safety. Look there! The little red squirrel is scolding us for being so slow!"

They tried to make up for their rest by moving more quickly through the tangled growth and clumps of moss-covered boulders. Every now and then the sound of the sea came to them on the wind, the far boom of waves crashing on the shore.

In the late afternoon, Philippe, leading the way with Aimée on his back, stopped abruptly at the edge of a small clearing. The others, eyes on the ground for obstacles, tumbled into him.

"What is it?" Gaby whispered.

Jonas said nothing. Burdened willingly with Simon over his small shoulder, he stood, his dark eyes wide.

"There's something there!" Philippe whispered. "The ruins of a hut or cottage?"

Gaby followed him through the pine and aspen trees. She looked at the strange, low stone structure built into the side of a hill in a pine glade. It was overgrown with moss and creeping vines. She smiled, "I know what that is! An old limekiln!"

Jonas was between them. "Massa! Someone there?"

Philippe put an arm around his shoulders. "I don't think so, Jonas. It hasn't been used in quite a while by the looks of it. It's an old limekiln, as Gaby says, where limestone was burned to make the quicklime used in the mortar between the building blocks of the fortress. But I have another use for it. We could spend the night here and have a little shelter."

"What about the fumes from the kiln?" Gaby worried. "Won't they be dangerous?"

"I don't think so. It hasn't been used for a long time, look at the moss and creeping vines. We could curl up in the sunken passageway that was used to feed the fire and get the burnt lime out. We'll feel safer that way."

They moved closer. Philippe held up a hand in warning. "The vines are broken at the entrance. Someone's been here."

Another voice, harsh, demanding, rose above his. "Don't move closer! I'll strike!"

Philippe dared to peer in. Crouched in the corner was the very soldier whose face had appeared at his hiding place in the wall! Fisherman's clothes had replaced his uniform. His club, made from a heavy tree branch, was ready to strike.

Philippe knelt at the tunnel entrance. "Monsieur, we're running away as you are. We're taking this young slave with us. Don't you think we need safety as you do?"

The soldier half rose, and pointed his club at Jonas. Jonas froze in terror. "What are you doing with the cobbler's slave?"

Philippe thought quickly. "We need everything we can bargain with, Monsieur. He might fetch a good price when the British take over the fortress!" *God forgive him for that!* "Monsieur, how did you know this place was here?"

"My buddies and I found it when we were out gathering spruce boughs to make sapinette. I'd planned to meet one of them here."

Gaby broke in, "You can share our food and water, Monsieur."

"I could do with that." The soldier made room for them in the tunnel. "It'll help me get on my way faster."

Philippe saw his face was haggard, seamed with an old wound. "Here, then, eat and drink a little with us. I know you were a soldier. Are you in the regular army?"

"No. I was forced to join. At least here I can sleep on spruce boughs, free from vermin and the drunken sot I had to share a cot with." He spoke thickly, jamming handfuls of food into his mouth and gulping water. "I wanted to marry a fisherman's daughter. Her father wouldn't allow it. Now we'll never see one another again."

So that's where the fisherman's clothes had come from, the girl!

Philippe spoke urgently. "The British have come ashore. I think you'd better make more distance between yourself and the fortress. You could be shot by the French as a deserter or by the British as a spy."

The man scrambled to his feet. "I didn't know they'd made it on to the shore. You're right. I can't wait. I'd better get away from here. I can travel till it's really dark. I think I'll head for Fourchu."

"Then take some of our food with you." Gaby made a small bundle and handed it to him. "Drink as we do from the streams."

Without any word of thanks he was gone, the need for flight putting wings to his heels. Then they were alone in the kiln's tunnel.

There was room for all of them in the kiln, and with the tunnel walls for shelter, they felt safer than they had at any time since their escape from the fortress.

"We need more moss to change the babies." Gaby removed their soiled underclothing.

"There's lots around here. I'll fetch it now." Philippe gathered it from the rocks and gnarled tree trunks beyond the kiln and filled the flagon with water from a small stream, babbling noisily nearby.

After eating, like animals in a hidden den, again they curled up for warmth with one another, and slept like the dead with exhaustion.

In the early dawn, Philippe was the first to wake. There had been a high sound on the morning air. It came again, a chorus of howling. Gaby and Jonas, alarm on their faces, struggled to wake.

"No need to fear," Philippe said. "It's wolves and that

means we've covered a good distance from the fortress. Can you still hear echoes of the battle?"

They listened. The echoes muted by distance and fog, were still there. "We can travel more freely," Philippe decided. "Tonight we'll make a fire. I don't think it'll be seen now, and it'll give us some comfort and warmth in the damp night."

While they ate from Gros Raymond's bag, Gaby looked at its contents and at what was left of the dead British soldier's rations. "The food's getting low," she said. "We'll have to find more."

Jonas, listening, handed her his portion of breakfast.

Philippe smiled at him. "No, Jonas, no need for sacrifice yet. We'll gather some edible roots as we go along, maybe some bulrushes, and we can find some wild strawberries, too. As long as we keep within the sound of the sea, we're in no danger of getting lost in the forest."

In mid-afternoon they broke into a small clearing beside a steeply-stepped pool. There were waist-high ferns and the hum of bees. "Like paradise after the battle." Gaby sank to her knees, and lowered Simon to the ground. "Couldn't we have a longer stay here to rest?"

"We could and I'll look for some fish in the pool for supper."

"There are still some petticoat rags left," Gaby advised. "You could use one of the larger ones as a net."

Relief in his heart that they had made it so far without pursuit, Philippe made his way down to the water. Surely Jonas would be safe with them now. The loud splash when it came, startled him to a stop. *What was that? Someone fording the stream?* He ducked behind a bush and waited.

Another loud splash! *Someone big and heavy then, to disturb the water so.* He took a deep breath and dared to peer out of the bush. *Another splash* — beaver! A beaver, finishing the dam that had made the pool, had sensed his presence and was warning his family with a mighty thwack of his broad tail on the water!

Philippe laughed aloud in his relief. "Thank you for the pond, Monsieur Beaver!" he said. "I hope you've made it possible to find some fish there!"

The Cry in the Night

The beaver pond was, indeed, home to fat trout, and in the petticoat net Philippe caught several of them. They cooked them on a fire, easily made with so much kindling and many dead branches available. They had a feast with trout, bread, lard and wild strawberries.

"Like a banquet," Gabrielle said and knelt to give thanks for the blessing.

The children were overcoming the effects of the herbs and watched, with delight, the squirrels scampering up and down the nearby birches.

"There are flying squirrels in the forest, too," Gaby told Jonas. "But they come out only at night from their nests in the trees, so don't be afraid if you hear one over your head in the dark."

But Jonas, his small thin body overcome with the stress of travel, the fear of discovery and helping to carry the babies, fell deeply asleep after supper, his arm flung across Simon.

Gaby and Philippe sat close to the fire, almost asleep themselves, but relishing the moment of peace that seemed at last without danger.

Gaby looked up suddenly. "What was that?" she whispered.

"You heard something?"

"A cry! I thought I heard a cry."

"Some animal likely, Gaby. This is the time when many of them come out for food and water."

Comforted, Gaby put her hands to the fire. "Philippe, shall I ever see Louisbourg again?"

"Perhaps not. If the British win this time, that will be the end of it." How strange to feel only sadness at this thought, where once his British blood might have counted it a victory. "When did the siege really begin?"

"It seems a long time ago. June the first was our yearly festival, celebrating the Blessed Sacrament. We all looked forward to it." Her face shone in the firelight. "There was to be a fine procession of the clergy and all the important citizens of our town. We made tapestries and hung them out to add to the splendour. And all the ships in the harbour had to fly special flags." She paused, the joy gone from her face.

"And?"

"We woke to hear that the British fleet was sailing again towards our harbour."

"Again? They'd been here before?"

"Oh, yes. They've blockaded the harbour entrance for the past three summers and we often went hungry when no food ships came in. The Indians brought us venison and bear meat —" She stopped suddenly, puzzled. "I heard it again!"

"You mean the cry?"

"Yes, Philippe, the cry!"

Philippe listened. "I hear nothing, Gaby. Are you sure you're not just being anxious?"

"Perhaps. It's hard not to be. But it sounded like a human voice."

"Probably a baby raccoon then. There's nothing sounds more like a child crying than that." He prompted her to keep remembering. "So you went ahead with the celebrations anyway?"

"Oh, yes. We waved our flags, and the procession wound through the streets and the guns fired salutes from the bastions." She tried to sound brave. "That will be the last Feast Day in Louisbourg."

He put a gentle arm around her shoulders and held her close. "Gabrielle, all that's behind us now. We'll sleep soundly and be on our way again to Luc Gabon's in the morning." He added as an afterthought, "And don't worry about cries in the night. Our fire will keep away creatures who hunt in the dark."

Gaby had fallen asleep and Philippe was drifting off in reasonable comfort when the cry came again. It did sound human. He waited but heard nothing more. Like the others he was too tired to keep a vigil. He slept.

They awoke early to a rising wind. Philippe lit a small fire to warm them, cooked more of the fish for a quick breakfast and filled the flagon at the pond. Then they were on their way, keeping to the sound of the sea. The morning fog thickened but they found another deer trail that made their going less dangerous.

The cry when it came again was so close Philippe almost fell over a huge boulder in the path. "That's no raccoon, Gaby, that's a human voice!"

They all looked at one another in fear and wonder. Jonas, Aimée on his back, pointed suddenly. "Look, Massa! The ground goes down!"

Philippe moved forward slowly. The ground *did* go down. It was a stone quarry on their right. They could have fallen into it in the fog, if they hadn't been on the deer path.

They listened again but heard nothing. Philippe made a decision. "I'll have to go down. It could be someone fallen as we might have done."

"But what if it's a British soldier?" Gaby said. "He could shoot you!"

"I think if he were wounded he wouldn't put up a fight. And remember, I speak English." He turned to Jonas. "Keep them safe here, Jonas, while I'm gone."

"Yes, Massa. Safe. Go careful."

It was the only way he could go. The path down was hazardous. It was obvious the quarry had been long abandoned. Small trees had taken root in the crevices and vines crept over the surface to entangle his feet. Then there were the stone projections and ledges, hard to see in the fog. But it was under one of them he did see something. A movement, a splash of blue in the thick light. Noiselessly, with great caution, he moved towards it. Then as he kept his eye on the ledge, a face appeared at its edge. *A child's face! Emilie's! How could this be? How in the world could she get to this place?*

She had seen him. She cried out, wrenching sobs punctuating her words. "You! I know you! You came for me!"

"No, Emilie. I didn't know you were here." He clambered down beside her under the ledge and gathered her in his arms. "There now, child, you're safe with us. We've found you!"

"I can't be safe anywhere!" The wild crying went on.

"There was fire and people dying and the nunnery was hit. Why did I ever want to leave it? I'll never be safe again!"

"You're safe with us. Come now, I'll help you to the top and you'll find friends."

He guided her, still sobbing, to the quarry's edge. The others stood there, mouths agape in wonder.

"Poor lamb!" Gaby took her at once and folded her in her arms. "Whoever can she be?"

"Oh, I know who she is," Philippe said. "This is Emilie, an orphan from the nunnery."

"But how did she get here," Gaby said, "all alone?"

"Not alone." Emilie's voice was muffled against Gaby's shoulder. "I'd never come out here alone. Antoine brought me!"

Of course! Antoine! Just as he'd promised, thought Philippe. "And where is he now, Emilie?"

"I don't know. I don't know. I went to follow a pretty bird and when I turned around he was gone and I couldn't find my way." She started sobbing again. "Oh, please, let me go back! I won't mind about all the needlework and the saints and the prayers! I'll learn them all. I don't like it here. Just let me go back. Please let me go back!"

They all sat down on the rough boulders. Philippe turned Emilie's face to his. "Emilie, there's no going back. There won't be anything to go back to when the British have finished."

"There won't? Nothing?"

"Nothing for us and the likes of you. But you can come with us. We'll look after you." He wondered how he could manage to make the food last. It would mean more searches

81

for roots, berries and last year's nuts. He looked into the small thin face. "How did you get down there?"

"I climbed down. I used to climb the trees in the garden when the Sisters weren't looking."

"Did you think you'd be safer there in the quarry?"

"Oh yes, safe from all the funny noises and the big eyes in the dark."

"You were clever to do that, Emilie. Now you're hungry. You've been down there a long time. Gaby will find some food and water for you."

Emilie forgot her tears in her eagerness for food, stuffing the leftover fish and bread in her mouth like some small wild animal.

Jonas watched, fascinated by this child in clothes almost as ragged as his own. He took her hand when she'd finished. "Massa, I look after her. No more going away."

"You do that, Jonas. It's time for us to move on. Remember, follow the deer trail and always listen for the sound of the sea."

When an occasional sun broke through the fog they searched beside the track for more wilderness food and stuffed the bags with hickory nuts and berries. As long as they had water they were content and Isle Royale bubbled with fresh water streams and waterfalls. They stopped by one for lunch, watching as they ate, the deep cascade foaming over a wide outcropping of rock. It was to be their salvation. They heard the voices as they ate wild berries cupped in their hands.

"Singing!" Gaby whispered. "A French song! Who is

singing?"

Philippe motioned her and the rest to silence. "French soldiers," he warned. "On their way from an outport to join the fortress garrison." He made an instant decision. "Jonas, see that waterfall? Go right through the water and behind it."

"Behind it, Massa?" Fear spoke in every word.

"Yes, behind it! There's a space in the rock like a cave behind the fall. Go there at once through the water and stay till we call you! And you, Emilie, not a word!"

Jonas didn't stay to argue. He plunged through the water and disappeared from view. The others turned away to face the path before them. Only a moment later the soldiers, in their ragged blue and white uniforms, broke through the glen of hickory and oak trees and tumbling over one another, stopped in amazement.

"Ho! Ho! What have we here?" The big fellow at the head of the small ragged column spoke first.

Philippe replied boldly. "Refugees from the battle, Captain. I'm taking them to safety from the shelling."

"And where can you take them in this wilderness?" The men behind him agreed with his doubt, murmuring among themselves.

"You'll all die of starvation!" one shouted.

"No, my friends," Philippe assured them. "We're going to a relative in Gabarus on the other side of the bay. These are all orphans, one from the nunnery, the others, children of a fisherman who drowned some time ago. I think we'll make it even if our supplies are small."

"Well, we can help you out there," the captain turned to his followers. "A little from each of your backpacks, men. We have plenty to go on. Jean-Paul, you pass a sack around."

There was a general turn-out of bread, cheese and meat into a small sack, as the soldiers looked with pity on Philippe's charges. "We've come from Fort Toulouse." Another man with a careworn face spoke up. "We saw a great flash a while back. What could that be?"

"The King's Bastion was hit with shelling," Philippe told them. "But our men are returning fire with fire. The battle's not lost." Philippe knew it wasn't true, but spoke to reassure them.

"Captain," Jean-Paul spoke, "why don't we stop here and refresh ourselves at the pond and waterfall? We're an unsightly mess after crawling through all that bush!"

Philippe could sense the others, like himself, tremble with apprehension.

"It hardly matters how we look, Jean-Paul." The captain was brusque. "What matters is that we get to the fortress fast. They'll need all the men they can muster. On our way now and Godspeed to you, young man, and your charges. Safe journey!"

"For you, good Captain, too!" Philippe stood silent with the others, watching the soldiers, muttering disappointment, disappear through the grove of balsam. He motioned them all to silence until the last sound of tramping feet had finished echoing back to them.

"Poor fellows," Gaby whispered. "They're not much better off than we are. Some of the soldiers were prisoners in France, and were forced to serve out their sentences here."

Emilie spoke at last. "I was quiet, wasn't I? I didn't say one word! Not one word!"

"Not one, Emilie!" Gaby hugged her. "The Sisters at the nunnery would have nothing but praise for you."

"And for Jonas!" Philippe slid down to the waterfall. "Jonas, we're safe! You can come out now!"

They all waited beside the pond. There was no answer. No Jonas!

Philippe frowned. "What could have happened to him?" He couldn't have drowned. It was only a waterfall he had to go through.

"Where is he?" Gaby's voice trembled

Philippe called again. There was still no answer. "I'm going to find out. Watch the others, Gaby. I'll be safe." He plunged headlong through the cascading water and was soaked at once to the skin. In the dim light beyond the water he saw a huge fold in the rock that stretched into darkness. "Jonas! Jonas, where are you?"

"Massa! Massa! I here!"

Oh, praise all the Saints! He was here somewhere! He was safe!

"Jonas, the soldiers have gone! You can come out now!"

On hands and knees, he came from behind a massive boulder. Stricken, he looked at Philippe. "Massa, I hear them say they come to the water. I hiding!"

"Wise Jonas! Come now. We've both got to get out of here and make a fire to dry our clothes."

They took them off in the underbrush and wrapped themselves in the old blankets while Gaby strung their clothing on branches close to a roaring blaze.

"We'll stay here for the night," Philippe decided. "We'll feed the babies well, then give them more of Gros Raymond's herbs, so they'll sleep well too. We'll rest up for the journey ahead."

The clothes dried and the blankets laid on balsam branches, they ate and then sat around the fire, wordless, exhausted by the afternoon's adventure. Emilie, trying to keep her eyes open, cried out suddenly. "Antoine! I want Antoine! Where is he?"

"Out there looking for you, little one," Philippe assured her. "We'll probably find him on the way."

"But I want him now! He promised we'd be together and he'd be my father and I wouldn't have to learn all about the Saints or sit in a corner any more, because I was bad." Emilie began to cry, her face a mask of misery.

"And you won't have to, we promise, Emilie." Gaby hugged her until the sobs ceased and Emilie slept. They laid her on the boughs and covered her with a blanket. Jonas was asleep beside her in a moment.

Philippe and Gaby sat silent, staring at the flames. Gaby spoke softly, "Do you think we shall, Philippe?"

"Find Antoine, you mean? I don't know. It's so easy to get lost in the forest unless you keep by the sea as we're doing." He glanced towards the sleeping Emilie. "Poor little one. She's had enough trouble without losing hope for the future."

"Have we any hope for the future, Philippe?"

"Gaby, we must never give up hope. We're away from the danger of battle at least, even if there are other dangers yet to be faced." He saw her staring into the darkness as she rose to check on the babies. "What's the matter?"

"Oh, nothing, I guess. I just thought I saw a light."

"A light? Where?"

"Over there in the west. It seems to flicker, to move around."

Philippe didn't want her to be anxious. "Come and sit by the fire. There's no one out there. I'm sure. Tell me about life on Isle Royale." That at least would keep her from fear.

Gaby smiled at him. She knew what he was about. "It's all right, Philippe. I haven't lost my courage. What would you like to know?"

"About the little settlements along the coast. Do they all fish for cod?"

"Most of them but some gather stone and timber for rebuilding the fortress. It's always in need of work what with the damage done in the British siege of '45 and the weather and ocean salt. Salt's our enemy."

"Except when you use it to salt down the cod to send overseas." *What was that light?* Even he could see it now, flickering strangely through the trees.

"You see it, don't you?" Gaby stared into the distance.

"It's probably only reflection from the shelling at the fortress. Light does strange things in fog." Determined to ignore it, he returned to the subject of life on Isle Royale. "There isn't much farming done here, is there?"

"Some on the Mira River but many of the outports trade cod for flour, oats and meat, with ships from New England."

"And now they're enemies in battle." Philippe stood up suddenly. "Gaby, there is a light! I have to know what it is. It could mean danger for Jonas or for all of us." He glanced at the small ones huddled together under the blankets. "You'll be all right here?"

Gaby looked nervous. "Of course. But come back quickly. The forest makes me afraid, after those soldiers. I'll gather up our supplies in case we have to leave suddenly."

Leave suddenly is what Philippe did, creeping in the near dark over twisted branches and moss-covered logs. Animals on night prowls, scuttered on his path. Several times his face was stung by bent tree branches, making his going noisier than he wanted. The closer he came to the light, the more his puzzlement grew. Could it be a soldier's encampment? Surely it was too faraway from the battle for that but mysterious and frightening nonetheless. He drew closer, crawling on hands and knees. The light danced. *What could it be?*

Carefully, silently, he parted the intertwined alder branches and gaped. A bog! It was a bog alight with fireflies! Thousands of them! The air above the ground-hugging bog bushes fluttered and whirled with light. He bent to examine the plants at his feet. Cranberries! But not ripe enough to eat. He gazed entranced at the spectacle of dancing light then turned to make a swift return to his charges. He stumbled and fell. His hand felt something as he tried to get back on his feet. *A leg!* He must have stumbled over a body! Then he saw it, half-sprawled across a huge fallen oak branch. Was it a soldier? No, there was no uniform, only a worker's clothing torn by brambles. The man groaned. Philippe crept closer to see his face. Antoine! It was Emilie's Antoine! God and all the Saints be praised!

"Stop Or I'll Shoot"

It was Antoine — but what was the matter with him? Philippe shook the man gently. "Antoine! Antoine!"

The other started up, holding his head in agony. "I'm not a deserter. Believe me, I'm not! Don't shoot!"

"I have nothing to shoot with, Antoine. Look at me!"

The man, his face grey with illness, stared at Philippe. He tried to focus his eyes, glazed and suffering.

"You know me, Antoine. Remember?"

Hope suddenly lit up the other's face. "You're the one Emilie talks about. I met you at the nunnery."

"That's right, I'm Philippe. What's the matter? Are you ill?"

"I was hungry. I ate some berries. I think they poisoned me. I vomited everything up but I'm still weak and dizzy."

"You're lucky to be alive. Come! We'll get you back to our little camp and give you fresh water and rest."

"But what about Emilie! She's lost and she'll die!"

"Oh, no she won't, Monsieur! We found her, too, down a stone quarry!"

"You found Emilie?" Antoine, his shoulders heaving with sobs, collapsed on the oak branch. He tried to regain his composure. "I'm sorry. I thought I'd never see her again."

"You will, Monsieur, and soon. Come, let me help you back to the fire and some comfort. Emilie's asleep but we'll wake her and let you rejoice together."

And what rejoicing! Antoine hugged the sleepy child to his body, crooning over her as if she were a baby.

Before they all slept, they made Antoine drink plenty of water from the falls, then made a place for him next to Emilie. "Rest well, Monsieur." Philippe covered them with a blanket. "We'll talk in the morning."

Quiet, too, had covered them when he heard Gaby's whisper. "Philippe, you didn't tell me what the light was!"

"Fireflies, Gaby." His voice was sleepy. "Fireflies in a cranberry bog."

Emilie was awake first with a shout of joy. "It's Antoine! I didn't dream it! It's him! Philippe, do you see? It's Antoine!"

"I do see, Emilie, and I'm happy too." He roused the others to bathe at the stream, have a light meal and prepare for the journey ahead.

Antoine was firm in his decision. "I'm stronger now. I'm going to take Emilie and be on my way."

"Where to, Monsieur?" Gaby asked. "Wouldn't you be better to stay with us?"

"I have plans, Gabrielle. I'm going to travel on trails that run behind the fortress and the fighting and head for the Mira River."

"Why there, Antoine?" Philippe was bundling the sleeping babies in the backpacks.

"The Brothers of Charity who run the hospital have a farm there. They raise crops and animals to feed the patients."

If there's a hospital left, Philippe thought grimly.

"You'll find work then and shelter?" Gaby said.

"I hope, or in the shipbuilding going on there. At least I can keep Emilie away from the shelling." He turned to Philippe. "Why don't you come, too?"

"Thank you, Monsieur. But I think it's best for us to find our way to Luc Gabon's farm. There'll be help there for all of us."

They gave him food for the journey and stood watching silently as the two made off deeper into the forest.

Emilie turned once, tears streaming down her face.

"Godspeed, Emilie!" Gaby called. And then they were gone.

They travelled on themselves, weary with the never-ending journey. Now and then they stopped to find last year's nuts left by squirrels in tree cavities, sometimes berries by a stream. It was by one of these they stopped again. "Our food's running low after the sharing," Philippe said. "I'll take the old petticoat net and cast for more fish."

The others came to join him beside the water. He cast again and again but this time there was no catch. "That's odd," Philippe said. "This stream in such a wild place should be full of salmon or trout. It's too far from the fortress for fishermen."

But there were other fishers. He put his finger to his lips and pointed. Upstream, a few yards from where they fished was a huge black bear, feeding two cubs. They'd been fishing, too!

Jonas clung to Philippe's ragged jerkin. "They see us! They eat us!"

"We must get back into the trees. Go quietly. Not a word."

But the bear had scented them. She began to lumber

towards them, sniffing warily. She would protect her young. Philippe tore apart the undergrowth to help them escape. As the others scrambled and gasped, Philippe looked back. "It's all right," he whispered. "She's returned to her cubs. Go easily but quickly."

They stumbled over fallen and dead branches and out-crops of moss-covered rocks until they found an animal track not too far from the cliff edge. An early morning fog near the sea was lifting and a watery sun was making the going easier. There were some huge boulders in a small clearing, making a protected private place in their midst. "This is perfect," Philippe said. "I'm going to leave you here."

"Leave us?" Gaby looked alarmed. "Where are you going?"

"Down the cliff. I know the Basque fishermen cast nets all along the shore. I think I can see some drying racks down there. There may be fish left on them. Jonas will you look after Gaby and the little ones while I go?"

"Yes, Massa." He tried to look brave. "Always, Massa."

"Good, and Gaby, the babies are stirring. Why don't you change them with the moss here and let them move around between the boulders while I'm gone?"

"I could do that, but oh, Philippe, do go carefully. What would I do on my own?"

"You don't need to even think about it. I'll be back as soon as I've had a look down below."

He waved to them cheerfully as he edged over the cliff and began to worm his way down among the rocks, crumbling earth and the shrubs hardy enough to root there. He stopped short halfway down, and stared. He could hardly believe such good fortune. Not only were there remnants of dried fish on the racks, there was a fisherman's hut on the beach and a small dory drawn up before it! There would be more food and shelter for a long safe rest for the night.

He returned swiftly up the cliff to the sound of waves crashing on the shore. He told them of his find.

Gaby eyed the babies. "Can we get down safely?"

"If we take it slowly. I'll go first, Jonas after and we'll get the babies on to solid ground first."

"I can make my own way down," Gaby told them. "I've done lots of climbing."

With the shelter for the night in view, they went slowly and happily, careful of every step. At the bottom Gaby saw the dory. "Philippe! A boat! We could row the rest of the way!"

"Too dangerous, Gaby. We're better to keep hidden where neither British nor French can see us. We'll have a look at the hut first to see if we can make it comfortable for a good night's rest."

They moved to the door, hanging crookedly half off its rope hinges, Philippe with Simon on his back, Aimée on Jonas's and Gabrielle behind them.

Philippe had his hand on the door to swing it wide when a loud shout made him fall back against Jonas.

"Stop! Or I'll shoot! Stop, I say!" *English! An English command!*

They stood crowded together. Philippe's whisper broke their total silence. "I'm going to look in. Stay there!" He crept closer to the door again and tried to peer in. What looked like a pool of blood lay in the corner.

"Didn't you hear me? Don't move! Don't come near me. I have a musket!"

Philippe's legs trembled. He kept his voice firm, unwavering. He knew now part of the pool of blood was the scarlet of a British solder's uniform. "Captain!" he called in English. "I'm British like you! Can't you hear me speak?"

"You've come to capture me and shoot me. I warn you, don't try any tricks on me. You'll be dead in a minute! And, don't move from that door! You'll be off to get help to take me prisoner."

"Sir, I haven't come to play tricks or take you prisoner." Philippe wished he could see the man's rank. It was too dark inside. "I and my family are running away from the battle. You must have been wounded to seek shelter in here."

"What's that to you?"

Philippe motioned the others farther back. His heart hammering, he moved closer to the door. "Sir, if you're wounded, you need help. We'll give it to you if you'll let us come in."

"I said, 'don't move'! There's lots of shot left in this musket!"

"Sir, I'm not moving. I'm not going anywhere! Can't you hear my speech? It's English like yours!"

The soldier groaned in pain. "Many a man can speak English. They learn it in trade. That's how spies are born."

"Sir, you've likely crawled a long way from the battle to find safety. If you're wounded you need help. If you put down your musket we can give you that help."

"Or overcome me and drag me back to the fortress to be shot."

"Never! Sir, my father, like you, is in the British army. His name is Lieutenant Richard Wyndham. Perhaps you know him."

"I've never heard of him. You're making it up. You're the enemy." He saw Philippe's hand on the door. "I told you, don't move or I'll shoot." But he sounded less decided.

"What's he saying?" asked Gaby. Philippe told her briefly, in French.

Gaby whispered, "I could tear up my last petticoat and bind his wounds."

There was another shout, edged with pain. "I knew it, French! I heard that voice! And you said you were English!"

"And I am, Sir." Philippe took a deep breath and went through the doorway, his life in every step.

"Soldier, I have with me a French girl, her two baby siblings and a slave. I'm trying to get them away from the battle to safety. Does that sound like an enemy? If you don't let us in to help you, you'll starve to death in here."

There was silence, Philippe approached slowly. "Lay down your gun. My little family will come in and do all we can for you." He saw the pool of blood under the man's left leg. "You're badly wounded. You need the bleeding stopped."

"How can I trust you? How can I know you're not lying?" It was becoming more and more of an effort for him to speak. The musket wobbled dangerously in his hands.

"Why would I lie? I told you my father is British. I'll tell you a secret. I came here on a mission to find him. I lost all my family in Acadia." *Anything to get the man to lay down his musket.* "Let us help you."

Slowly, hands trembling, the soldier drew back the gun and placed it beside him. His eyes were filled with pain as Philippe and Gaby drew near. Jonas crept to a dark corner, the two little ones wailing beside him.

Gently Gaby lifted the soldier's leg and examined the gaping flesh. She took command. "Philippe, help me tear strips from my petticoat. Some I'll soak in the ocean salt water to cleanse the wound. Then I'll bind it tight to stop the bleeding."

She did as she planned, wincing at the soldier's cry of pain as she worked.

Philippe extended his arm. "Now can you stand? I know you're weak but try."

The soldier, leaning on them both, managed to get to his feet. Now it was Philippe's turn to give the orders. "If we help you, you can get back to your regiment. There's an old dory. One of the oars is partly broken but the other is sound enough. We'll get you in there and you can paddle your way towards the British fleet in Gabarus Bay. Do you think you're strong enough to do that?"

"I do! I can take it slowly. Let me see the surf."

They came to the ocean's edge, Jonas peering at them from the hut door. The soldier, in spite of his pain, was encouraged. "It isn't high today. And look! I can see our fleet away over there on the horizon! I can make it! I know I can!"

As he spoke they could see the far distant sky lit by the battle, explosions of light streaking the sky. "Come then, we'll help you into the dory and see you off." Philippe placed the soldier's tricorne hat in the boat beside him. "Better not wear that and be spotted by a French lookout. Keep low in the boat, and rest often."

"Philippe, I've made a small bundle of food." Gaby placed it in the boat. "He'll be stronger if he eats."

The soldier turned to them, his long fair hair and blue eyes grimed with sweat and dirt. "There's nothing I can do to thank you. Godspeed on your own journey."

"We'll make it safely and so will you." Philippe gave the dory a shove and it bounced on to the waves. The soldier began to paddle steadily, not looking back.

"And will he?" Gaby whispered.

"Find his way back to his comrades safely? We can only hope. We've done our best." And in a way he felt he'd done it for his father. "Now we'll make the hut clean and comfortable for a night's stay. We'll bury the blood with sand. We should have no fear now, down here on the shore in a hut at last."

A Strange Gift of Food

It was a luxury to have enough warm food to eat, to comfort themselves at the driftwood fire and seek sleep with four walls around them and the sound of the surf at their door. It was warmer inside than in the forest but they lay close, the babies between them, to preserve the heat of their bodies.

Still ill at ease from their encounter with the soldier, Philippe crept out from the blankets in the dark midnight.

Gaby woke. "What is it?"

"I thought I heard a sound."

"How could you? It's only the surf on the shore, rattling the pebbles."

"Probably." He listened again.

"What did you think it was?" Gaby whispered.

"The sound of rocks being dislodged by somebody climbing the cliff."

"You're on edge because of the soldier. He's gone now, Philippe, God with him, I hope. Come and sleep. Aimée needs you beside her to keep her warm."

Convinced, he crept under the blanket. There could be no one there. Fear was playing tricks with his imagination. They were safe and would soon be on their way again. He fell asleep at once.

When they wakened, drugged with exhaustion, the sun

was trying to pierce the fog. After a hasty breakfast they were off again, stumbling over roots and rocks. Sometimes they found an animal trail, more often they had to make their own but at least they didn't have to worry about the babies' chatter. There was no one this far from the fortress to hear. It was amazing how the little ones adapted to the strange daily trek and the nights of camping. Probably because they were always snuggled close to bodies, warm, dry and well-fed, even if the others had to cut back a little on their own food intake.

At noon they lit a fire to warm themselves, and again at night after a long gruelling day crawling under and over branches, always keeping within sound of the sea. Like many of their previous night shelters this one was surrounded by rocky ledges and huge boulders, cave-like in its protection. There was the usual bubbling stream for their water supply and plenty of broken branches for the fire. Gaby and Philippe sat close to it as the others slept, Jonas's arms flung across the babies.

Philippe was the first to break the silence. "Gabrielle, I think someone is following us."

Her eyes mirrored astonishment and fear. "You do? How do you know this?"

"It isn't a knowing, it's a feeling. I've had it all day."

"Why didn't you tell me?"

"I didn't want to alarm you unnecessarily, Gaby."

"But what makes you think so?" She moved closer to him. "What gives you this feeling?"

"Remember the sound on the cliff? I've heard more sounds, sometimes so small they're only on the edge of hearing."

"Philippe, it could be animals. We hear them out in the forest every night."

To punctuate her statement there came a wild cry in the darkness as some night rover found his prey.

"I know but this is different. It's like there's someone out there, keeping an eye on what we're doing."

Gaby stared fearfully into the darkness beyond their retreat. "Do you see anything now?"

"No, but that doesn't mean there isn't someone there."

"Philippe, who could it be?"

Philippe put a gentle arm around her shoulders. "Gaby, I can't imagine."

"Well, I can. Monsieur Dutot. He'll be in a terrible rage at losing Jonas."

Philippe looked thoughtful. "I don't think he believed my story about being your cousin from France either." Then he shook his head. "But to chase us this far seems even beyond our friend the cobbler."

"You don't know Monsieur Dutot. In a rage he's like a great bull, determined to get revenge on the British for killing his son. Jonas was his prized possession, someone he could vent his anger on and kick about as he pleased. He'd be outraged to know we'd stolen him from under his nose and made him look like a fool to his neighbours. And if he found out you were British ..." She had no need to finish. "Philippe, we have to hide. We really do."

"That isn't the answer. We're being watched now," Philippe told her. "I doubt that Monsieur Dutot could make his way quietly anywhere. His very rage would make him forget any need for caution."

But Gaby would not give up her suspicions. "It could be someone he hired then. He has plenty of money to offer a reward for his stolen property."

Philippe smiled ruefully. "We're not exactly equipped to put up a fight for him. Anyone he hired could have grabbed Jonas, and run."

Gaby was still insistent. "Perhaps he's undecided. I know the cobbler would never listen to our pleas for Jonas's freedom, but he may." Her face shone with animation. "If we could talk to this person, we might be able to persuade him how right we are."

"We could certainly try, Gaby." He smiled at her with admiration. "We'll stay in this protected area for two days and see if we can flush out our pursuer and face him with the challenge."

"You really think we could?" Hope rang in her voice.

"It's worth a try. It's reasonably dry in here and we can have a good rest for going on with the journey."

"And I can wash some of the clothes in the stream and dry them on the rocks. How about our food supply?"

"It's getting very low again. I'll try for more fish in the stream with the petticoat net. Now, Gaby, it's time for sleep. We need to keep the babies warm."

The sun did that for them the following day, drying the clothes and cheering their spirits. Philippe caught three trout and they grilled them at the fire, relishing them with a little leftover bread.

"Like a feast," Gaby said, "in our own little cave."

Philippe saw her eyeing fearfully the trees crowded around their camp. He said quickly, "Not as fine as the feasts at the fortress, they'd be something special."

"Oh, they were! We had many holy days for the apostles and the patron saints. On some we had to fast and hold prayer vigils all day. But the Festival of Saint Louis was the most important and it was a real feast day."

"Why for him?" Philippe moved casually to a place atop a tall ledge to enable him to better scan the surrounding forest.

"He was a King of France who was made a saint because of his crusade to the Holy Land. His festival came in August and we all had a holiday with lots to eat and the ships in the harbour firing their guns and flying their flags. The commandant even shared wine with us ordinary folk."

"And some drank too much?"

"Of course and there was drunkenness and brawls in the street. But it was a good, happy time." Gaby suddenly realized where she was. "And it'll never come again."

"Other good times will come." Philippe slipped down from his perch and turned to Jonas, listening open-mouthed to the story. "Keep an eye on them, Jonas. I'm going to scout around a little."

"Yes, Massa. Always, Massa."

With frightened eyes, Gaby watched him go but said nothing.

He crept quietly around the perimeter of the camp eyeing every tree as if it might come to life. He could see no sign of a human figure. There was a small trail that led off from their shelter, the one they would follow after their two days rest. He

glanced at the oak tree that towered at its entrance. He
stared. *What was that in the crook of one of the higher
branches?* He drew closer. It looked like a bundle wrapped in
animal skin. He stood on a rock at the base of the tree to
reach it and carefully lift it down. It was a skin, a rabbit skin.
He opened it to find portions of rabbit meat, bread and a
crude bark container of berries. He eyed it with astonishment. Where could it have come from?

When he raced back to the camp, Gaby and Jonas were
waiting and watching, faces tense and fearful. They looked in
wonder at the cache he'd found.

"Whose is it?" Gaby asked. "It looks quite fresh."

"A hunter's," Jonas said. "Massa, a hunter's."

"It could be, Jonas. A hunter going farther into the forest
and leaving food for himself for his return." He shook his
head. "But hunters don't usually do that. They eat what they
catch day by day and take the rest back to their cabins."

"Then what shall we do with it?" Gaby asked.

"Eat it, of course! We'll have our own feast-day by the fire!
If you like, we can have it in honour of St. Louis!"

And feast they did, the aroma of the meat cooking on the
fire making their mouths water. They saved enough for the following day and Gaby gave thanks on her knees for such good
fortune.

With Jonas and the children quickly asleep, their stom-
achs satisfied, Gaby said suddenly, "You've never told me of
your mother and the little ones who were sent to France."

"I know."

"Would you like to tell me?"

Philippe looked away into the dark forest as if he were trying to see times past.

"My mother was very beautiful. She had raven black hair,
like yours." He smiled suddenly, sadly. "And her eyes were so
blue and they seemed to know everything." He fell silent.

Gaby reached out to take his hand. "And the children?"

"Like you, I have a brother and sister, William, five and
Chantal, three. Before they were born, we lost two to fevers."
He shook his head slowly. "It all seems so long ago now, as if
I'd dreamed it."

"Your mother in Heaven will be so glad to know the little
ones are safe in France."

And what of my father? Philippe thought with a sudden
pang of guilt. Aloud he said, "We'll stay together now, no matter what happens. We belong together."

"Yes. No matter what happens."

Comforted, they slept soundly. They didn't see the figure
who came to the edge of the trees and stared down at them.
But Gaby must have heard a twig snap or the warning of some
inner voice. She reached across Simon to shake Philippe.
"Philippe! Philippe!" Her voice was a whisper. "Wake up! I
heard something."

Philippe sat up suddenly, scrambled to his feet and walked
carefully, defensively around the camp. There was no one
there. "If someone was there, he's gone," he said quietly.

"Who was it? What did he want?"

"I don't know. But he didn't harm us, that's the important
thing. Go to sleep, dear Gaby. There's nothing we can do, but
we must get our rest."

She lay down but was up again in a moment. "What was that?"

"Now I do know what that was, an animal snuffling on the other side of the rocks scenting our food. I have it safely protected. He's out of luck. Try to sleep now."

But even he lay wondering, as he heard the night sounds of insects and animals in the deep dark. *Who was out there? What was his intent?* There was no way he could know and sleep was all he could do now, trusting God and all the saints to keep them safe til morning.

The View From the Cliff

"I think we should all bathe today in the rock pool below our flowing stream," Gaby decided the next morning. "You two," she indicated Jonas and Philippe, "can take off your clothes and jump in beyond that clump of willows. Then I'll tend to the babies and myself in the same place."

It was like a holiday-time. They were refreshed from the cold clear water, well enough fed and rested that they were able to forget their fears for a while and make up a tossing game with the smaller stones from the crevices. Then, to amuse the little ones, Philippe took a burnt stick from the fire and drew pictures and faces on the rock surfaces. Gaby and Jonas each had a turn and the other two had to guess what the drawing represented. Some of the guesses brought laughter that for a time made them forget place and pursuer.

Then night came and, after prayers, they settled solemnly for rest, not knowing what it would hold. But nothing disturbed their sleep or safety.

His decision made, Philippe roused them early. "Let's not waste any more time worrying about a follower. We're getting closer now to Luc's."

They set off in good spirits, fog again slowing their progress but even fog was not enough to hide another find from Jonas's sharp eye.

"Massa, look!"

Philippe at the head of the file, stopped, alarmed.

"In the tree, Massa! I seeing!"

Philippe, past the tree, looked back. His gaze followed Jonas's pointing finger. There it was, another bag lodged in the crook of a tree! He brought it down carefully.

"More meat, bread and berries!" Gaby eyed the food with astonishment. "Whose is it?"

"Ours now," Philippe decided, "since there's no one else in view. It'll give us strength for the rest of the journey."

"If we're allowed," Gaby said. "This surely could be some ruse to entice us into a trap."

Jonas let Simon down to ease his back. "A trap, Massa? Dutot?"

Philippe shook his head. "No, not Monsieur Dutot. I'm sure of that now Jonas."

"What shall we do?" asked Gaby.

"Whoever is leaving it, we'll go on as we have before, just be thankful for any food we can find. We can't be too far from Luc Gabon's. We've covered miles from the fortress."

With renewed vigour from the food, they plodded on, scrambling over trees even more stunted and distorted by Atlantic gales than those on earlier paths.

"I think we're changing direction," Philippe said. "We can still hear the sea but there's an echo as if there's a cove near-by."

While they stopped to eat the meat they'd cooked for the trail, the babies squealed with delight when a red-backed mouse came to investigate. They went down to drink at the ever-present stream and watched a mink slithering along the bank and into the watery undergrowth at the stream's edge.

When Philippe saw a white-tailed deer appear and disappear just as suddenly, he announced, "Stay here. He seems to be going up a little rise. I'm going to see where his trail leads."

"Philippe, don't get lost. I don't like being without you."

"I won't be far. Take this chance to rest." The white rear of the deer was his beacon as he tried to keep up with the animal. Tramping through the mass of broken trees and huge boulders that the deer's legs easily overcame, he mounted a small slope.

Suddenly the deer disappeared. Philippe broke through the forest cover. He was standing on a knoll with the sea frothing far below him. Looking to his left he could see sudden vivid flashes of light on the far horizon. The battle, still in progress in all its fury, was far behind them. They had come many miles safely and he was thankful. When he glanced along the seashore to the right he could have shouted for joy. There, in the distance, in the midst of a clearing, well back from the shore, was a dwelling, small and log-built. Luc Gabon's! It must be! He strained to see the surrounds. Yes! There were the outbuildings, a small log barn and a smaller shed he remembered, and a log fence around the garden to keep out the wild predators.

He raced back to the others, shouting. "We're nearly there! We've almost made it! Come and see!"

"Come and see what?" Gaby was alarmed, then puzzled.

"Luc Gabon's, Gaby! I can see it from the clifftop!"

"Oh, Massa! I coming!" Jonas needed no further invitation. Philippe took Simon from him as he raced up the small hill. Gaby followed.

"There! Can you see it?"

They stared, overcome with relief and gratitude.

"We're so close, Philippe. Oh, I do thank God. The babies will be safe!"

Jonas stared as if at an apparition. "Massa, how long now?"

Philippe's smile was glowing. "Perhaps another day, if we have a good night's sleep tonight and start early tomorrow morning."

Gaby still looked uncertain. "And you're sure Monsieur Gabon will welcome us, Philippe?"

"Without a doubt. He took me in with no questions asked. His wife was just as kind. I was able to help them about the farm and house and we can do the same."

"And what then, Philippe? Shall we have to stay there for always?" Gaby asked.

"One day at a time, Gaby. At least we'll be far from the fighting, in a safe place to plan what to do next."

But Gaby, thankful though she was, was still troubled. Safety seemed assured, for now. But what of the future?

The Rage of a Storm

The immediate future held calamity. They had traveled so far without any and they were so close to their goal, Gaby was in despair when she woke to Aimée crying in the night.

"Philippe! Wake up!"

"What? What is it?" He tried to see in the darkness.

"Philippe, it's Aimée. She's burning up with fever! Oh, Philippe, I'm frightened."

All the weariness of the trip, the anxieties, the fears were in her voice.

Philippe took her hands in his. "Gaby, it's going to be all right! Children get fevers, and get over them. We'll look after her."

"Massa, what is doing?" Bewildered, Jonas wakened and sat up.

"Jonas, Aimée is ill. We don't know the cause but we'll have to get her down to the stream for water to cool her fever."

"I help, Massa. Tell me where."

"Stay here with Simon, Jonas, and keep him safe."

"Yes, Massa." In his voice was his determination to be brave, for the sake of the smaller boy in his charge.

There was still light from the fire they had used to cook supper. Philippe carried the crying Aimée closer to it. When Gaby began to remove her clothes, Philippe gaped in astonishment. "Gaby, it isn't a fever. She's not ill! Somewhere where we've camped she's crawled into a patch of poison plant. Look at the rashes on her body!"

"But we have nothing to stop the burning! Gros Raymond's herbs won't do that!" Gabrielle tried to comfort the wailing child.

"I know something that will! It'll be growing alongside the plant that gave her the rash." Philippe lit two torches from the embers of the fire. "Jonas, you come with me, back along the path we've covered. We're looking for a three-leaved, shiny plant close to the ground. And we need a sack to bring back our find."

Jonas, aware of frightening animal eyes and sounds as they went, trailed along as close to Philippe's heels as he dared. For him, the forest was a place of mystery and danger but he kept his eyes steadily on the ground, determined to be the finder of the offending plant.

He was. It was in a small grove where they had previously stopped for Simon to relieve himself. "Massa, look! I finding!"

"Jonas, you're a jewel, just like the plant we'll find here!" Philippe made straightway for a patch of weeds with tall broad leaves. It was still blooming with irregular, showy flowers. "Pick the leaves, not the flowers, Jonas, and stuff them in the sack. But stay away from the poison plant!"

"Yes, Massa." Jonas stopped his intense harvesting suddenly. "Massa, I hearing."

"It's nothing, Jonas. Just the night sounds of the forest. Lots of animals come out to feed at night."

"Feed, Massa?" His eyes grew even more alert. "Massa, I

hearing growling!"

Philippe stopped his gathering, held his torch high to survey the dark woods. "I can't see anything!"

"There! Again!" Jonas stood straight and brave. "I not afraid, Massa, but I hearing."

Philippe smiled down at him. "Jonas, there's nothing wrong with your hearing. That's the rumble of thunder far off to the west."

They began their vigorous picking again and, the sack packed tightly with jewel-weed leaves, they hastened back to the little camp. Simon slept on soundly while Gaby rocked the still crying Aimée. The crying was muted almost at once as they took turns, squeezing the juice of the welcome weed over Aimée's rashes.

"It's like a miracle!" Gaby said.

"A miracle taught me by the Indians who befriended me on my way here, Gaby. But we have to make the miracle ourselves by keeping the jewel-weed juice on her body."

By the time Aimée fell asleep, they, too, were drained and drenched with sweat from the humid heat that now filled the glade where they camped. They slept the sleep of sheer exhaustion.

Thunder woke them in the morning to a day filled with stillness and almost unbearable heat.

After they'd eaten, fed the children and treated Aimée, they rolled her gently in a blanket for carrying and further treatment on their way. Philippe went to look up at the sky from the bank of the nearby stream. "It's getting very dark," he said. "A bad storm's coming. We'd best get going quickly."

"This is the first one we've had," Gaby said. "Lots of rain and fog but no storms."

"We've been lucky," Philippe smiled at her, "or blessed. But we've got to find a place to shelter out of it when it comes."

They plodded on, trying to ignore the threat of the ominous sounds growing in volume.

"Could we make a kind of shelter with tree branches, Philippe?" Gaby hugged Aimée closer every time a rumble swept over their heads.

"What if there's a high wind? What if there's a lightning strike? We could be in great danger. No, we'll have to find something better than that." *But what?* He wondered. *And where?*

Jonas saw the sign first. He stopped to stare. "Massa, look! On the tree!"

They all stopped and looked. It was an arrow daubed on the trunk with some dark rust-coloured wild root. Jonas was ahead of them. "Massa, Massa, look! Another!"

There was another, pointing away from the path, deeper into a dark copse of pine and balsam.

Gaby said, "What does it mean?"

"I don't know but you stay here," Philippe said "and I'll follow it to find out." He saw two more arrows before he discovered where they led. He raced back to the others. "Our guardian angel is still watching over us," he shouted. "The arrows point to a huge jumble of boulders. There's space enough for us to hide from the storm!"

As the first drops of rain began to fall, they arrived at the shelter and crept in thankfully. "It's like the one we stayed in for two days after we met the British soldier," Gaby said, "but bigger. Who knew this was here?"

"We may never find out," Philippe said. "It's a mystery." *Like the caches of food*, he thought.

Whoever had pointed the way, they were grateful. Gaby murmured prayers of thanks, as the thunder grew in intensity, and the lightning flashed so closely it lit up the rock interior that sheltered them. Then came wind and torrents of rain. As the storm grew more threatening, they huddled together for comfort, and said nothing. It seemed the barrage of light and sound would never stop. There was a strange sizzle, a blinding flash and an instant smell of burning. A great crash echoed through the forest. They all clung more closely to one another.

"It's a tree," Philippe said. "The lightning's struck a tree! We're all right! We're safe in here."

The children were wailing with fright, Aimée almost recovered, burying her face in Gaby's arms, Simon seeking Jonas's.

Then, the thunderclaps became less violent, the lightning less frequent, the storm grumbling away into the far distance.

Philippe crawled to the entrance of the shelter. "It's over! It's cooler." Then he saw the victim, a huge pine tree split down the middle, the scorch marks blackening the exposed surfaces.

"A giant of the forest," Philippe said, "felled with one blow."

"It's sad," Gaby said. "It was a beautiful tree."

"And we were the lucky ones. We weren't underneath it!" Philippe pointed to a tiny pine shooting up through a layer of pine needles. "And we see one to take its place, even if we won't be here to see it grow."

"Where shall we be?" Gaby asked. "At Luc Gabon's?"

"For now," Philippe said. "Look, the sun's coming out from the clouds. We'll wait till the ground dries a little and then set out again. Luc's is too close for us to linger here."

The Figure Between the Rocks

"The ground is still very wet." The next morning, Gaby followed Philippe's lead, picking her way carefully among the trees.

"Tread very carefully," Philippe warned. "It's slippery."

His warning came too late. Even as he spoke, Gaby went down.

Setting Simon on the ground, Philippe was beside her in a moment. "Gaby!"

Gaby's face was lined with anxiety. "I can't get up, Philippe. My foot's caught between the rocks."

It took the full strength of both Philippe and Jonas to move the rock far enough to release Gaby's foot. But when she tried to stand she cried out in pain.

Philippe hid his concern. *So near to safety and now this!* He quickly reassured Gaby. They would bind the foot and stay for the day so that Gaby could rest it.

The glade they were in was quite suitable for camping. They made Gaby a bed of spruce boughs among the tall ferns and tried to keep cheerful. "What if we can't go on?" Gaby asked suddenly.

"We'll go on." Philippe finished the bandaging. "The ankle's badly swollen and strained but I don't think anything's broken. I know it's painful but you rest now and Jonas and I will tend the babies and prepare our food."

Jonas's thin face was pinched with worry. "Better tomorrow, Massa?"

"Yes, Jonas. Better tomorrow. You and I can carry the babies and help Gaby, too."

Concern for their predicament had banished all sense of joy at the discovery of Luc's cabin. Philippe tried to bring cheer by inviting them to join in French songs his mother had taught him. They were all glad when dusk came and they settled down to sleep. Surely tomorrow would bring some healing. Philippe gave Gaby a portion of the babies' herbs and she finally slept. He did, too, exhausted with the long journey and anxiety over Gaby and his adopted family.

By morning their hopes were a thing of the past. Even with the herbs, Gaby had spent a pain-filled, restless night and couldn't bear any weight on her foot when she awoke.

"Philippe, you'll have to go on and leave me here."

"Leave you here alone?" Philippe was aghast. "We could never do that!"

"But I could face it as long as you and Jonas got the babies safely to Luc Gabon's. Please, please, take them!"

"Not if we have to leave you alone. Never!" Philippe was adamant. "We have plenty of food and water in the flagon. We'll stay here another day to see if there's any improvement."

Mid-morning, Jonas crept to Philippe's side. "Someone there!" he whispered.

Philippe looked around. "Someone where?"

"Out there. In the trees. I seeing a face!"

"A face?" Philippe whispered, too.

"Yes! A face! Over there!" Jonas pointed a trembling finger. His voice shook. "Monsieur Dutot!"

Suddenly there was a loud swishing sound. *The pursuer, thrashing through bushes?* Transfixed, they stared at one another.

"What is it?" Gaby called, sharply, and it came again, followed by the creak of a tree branch.

"A face, Missy! It look over the rocks. Very dark, like mine."

"Very dark?" Philippe echoed.

"Yes, Massa, very dark face. I see it. I see it!"

There was an interval between two huge protective rocks. All at once there was a figure there.

Philippe put out an arm as if to protect the others. Who could it be? And what defence did they have against him? Could he and Jonas rush him, catch him off guard? Then what? Even if they overcame him, how could they bind him? Slowly Philippe moved closer to the silent, motionless stranger.

Then, he was rushing towards him, shouting his name. "Raoul, Raoul, my old friend, how did you ever get here?" He reached out a hand to grab one of the other's.

Gaby sat bolt upright. "An Indian!"

Philippe was so overcome he could hardly get the words out fast enough. "Gaby, it's my Micmac friend Raoul! He helped me on my way here!"

Jonas hugged the two babies closer and watched, eyes wide.

"But how *did* he get here?" Gaby stared, too.

Philippe drew the deerskin-clad young man into their

midst. His puzzlement was profound. "Yes, Raoul, what miracle brought you?"

The Indian stood tall, straight and solemn. "No miracle, Philippe. I came for you." His French was clear and unaccented.

"But I last saw you at the Micmac camp near Fort Toulouse, where you fed and sheltered me. You told me there, it was the French priest, Father Raoul, who took you in as a child and raised you."

"He did and he even gave me his name." Now Raoul's words were a torrent of Micmac. "As I grew older, some made me feel I no longer belonged there because I was Indian. I went back to my own people." Hesitating, he looked down at Gaby. "I didn't know if the mademoiselle would accept me. That was why, well-hidden, I kept an eye on your safety."

Philippe translated Raoul's words for Gaby.

She looked astonished. Her eyes blazed. "Accept him? In the British blockade, it was the Micmacs who saved us from starvation by bringing us venison and bear meat and eels. When the British captured our ships and tried to burn down the outports, the Micmacs drove them away!" She reached up and seized the Indian's hand. "Thank you. Thank you!"

"How did you know where we were?" Philippe still wondered.

"I came, like many of my people to join the garrison in defending the fortress." Again Raoul spoke French.

"And yet you are here now?" Philippe said.

"As I arrived at the edge of the forest I saw you escaping. For me, your safety came first. I didn't know where you were going. There's danger in the wilderness for such as you're caring for."

Gaby stared at him. "You mean you've been following us all the way?"

"All the way. I intended to go back to the fortress, when I knew you had reached safety." He turned to Philippe. "Did you find your father, my friend?"

"No, Raoul, I found Gaby and her two babies and the slave. We wanted to get away from the fortress before it fell. It's been a difficult journey."

"And where does it end, Philippe?"

"For now, at Luc Gabon's. He's the farmer who took me in, as you did, on my way here."

Gaby's face shone. "It was you who left the food in the trees!"

Raoul nodded. "It was all I could do. I feared you'd starve. But then when I saw what happened," he looked down at Gaby's bandaged ankle, "I had to come and offer my help."

"You mean you'll see us safely to Luc's?" Philippe's relief was in his smile.

"I will. I can carry the mademoiselle on my back. You have enough to manage with the two babies."

Jonas still eyed Raoul fearfully. "Massa, all things good now?"

"Yes, good, Jonas. We'll make it to Luc Gabon's sooner than we thought." Raoul carried Gaby easily and the others, knowing that the Micmac would find the best and easiest way to go, followed. They travelled swiftly, silently, in good spirits.

When they stopped for food, Raoul shared news. "While I

was following you, I met some of my band coming from the fortress. They were going back to the Micmac camp to rouse more help."

"And what did they report?" Philippe asked. In his heart he knew the answer.

"The French have been driven from the entrenchments along the shore. Some of their artillery has fallen into British hands. Two French vessels escaped the blockade and are on their way to France."

How I wish we were on them, Philippe thought. Aloud he said, "They'll take news of the fate of the fortress?"

"I think so, my friend. And of their countrymen's valour and sacrifice, even tearing down their houses to repair the fortifications."

Philippe saw Gaby's sadness. "Remember, Gaby, we're on our way to a new life." What that would be, he had no idea. For the moment, Luc Gabon's was enough.

A Reunion — and a Surprising Encounter

The following day they came in sight of their longed for destination. They stood at the top of a small incline and looked down. There was Luc Gabon's cabin. Gaby and Philippe exchanged quick glances, neither quite believing they had reached the end of their fearsome journey.

There was no sign of anyone around the dwelling. Carefully they descended the hill. A flock of gulls on the sand and pebble beach screamed their annoyance at the intrusion as they flew to the ocean. A small dory was drawn up on the shore. "Monsieur Gabon fishes," Raoul said, "like most of us on Isle Royale."

But there was no Monsieur Gabon. They approached the cabin, log-walled and, like Gaby's, chinked with moss and mortar. Philippe, puzzled by the silence, Simon half asleep on his back, pushed wider the partly open door. The one large room with its hand-carved furniture, and fire burning on a stone hearth, was empty. A cradle, empty, too, stood in one corner.

Philippe felt a moment of panic. *Had the Gabons fled from the place, unable to face the hardships of life in the wilderness?*

Gaby spoke from Raoul's back. "I hear a cow. There must be someone here."

"They may be out gathering marsh hay for any cattle they

have." Raoul set Gaby on a chair near the fire. They all whirled at a sound from the door behind them.

"Luc!" Philippe set Simon on the floor, and rushed to grab his friend's hands in his own.

The man, tall, thin and gaunt-faced, for a moment was silent with astonishment. Joy in his voice, he spoke at last. "Philippe! How did you come?"

"With difficulty and danger, Luc." He turned to Raoul and the others. "Raoul is the Indian friend I told you about and the rest are now my family."

"And the fortress?"

"Fighting bravely but with little hope. We had to escape the shelling and we brought Jonas to escape a cruel master." Philippe still clung to his friend's hands. "Will you give us shelter, Luc, until we find what we're to do?"

"As long as you wish. Here the wilderness is your only enemy and we're taming that little by little."

Gaby spoke from her chair, "And what of Madame Gabon, will she object to our being here?"

Luc dropped Philippe's hands and looked with unbearable sadness towards the empty cradle. "My wife died in childbirth two months ago, and the baby with her."

The others were too stunned to speak. Raoul broke the silence, "Monsieur, we share your grief. My friends here will be company and help for you. As for me, I must make my way back to the fortress and join the defenders."

"And if the battle is lost to the British?" Gaby asked.

"If the battle is lost I shall return to my own people," said Raoul quietly.

"You must take more food to help you on your way." Luc set about packaging meat and bread from the larder.

"Thank you, Monsieur. And now it's time for my going. There are still many hours of daylight left for me to travel. I'll try to find someone who's acquainted with Gabrielle to tell them where you are."

"Look for Gros Raymond or the Monk," Gaby advised. "They're both well known at the hospital."

Raoul turned to Philippe, "And you, my friend, may the Great Spirit bring you and your new family the answers you need."

Philippe could say nothing. His eyes filled with tears, he reached out to embrace the Indian briefly. They stood at the door to watch him ascend the hill like a wild deer. With a last brief wave he was gone, swallowed by the forest.

Now, at last, with Luc Gabon, they found comfort and peace. The days passed in fog, rain and occasional sunshine and always the lightning fire of battle on the far horizon. It was joy for them to know the guns were faraway, to wake in the morning to a blazing hearth and the sound of the cock's crow and to realize the hardships and anxieties of the trail were behind them.

When the nights came, Gaby, with prayers of deep gratitude, rocked the babies to sleep in Luc's handmade cradle. Her lullabies gave them all a sense of home.

Jonas, once his uncertainties of Luc and his new surroundings were overcome, followed Luc about with obvious devotion as the farmer showed him the farm animals, the cow, several sheep, a goat, a flock of chickens and Jonas's favourite, a horse. "Brought over the trail from Breton Cove from a farmer who went back to France," Luc explained. He smiled down at Jonas. "How would you like to look after Belle, Jonas?"

"Belle?" Jonas looked puzzled.

"That's the horse's name. I'll teach you how to care for her."

"Oh, please, Massa! Please!"

"Good. She has to be fed and watered every day and given a good brushing. Do you think you can do that?"

"Oh, yes, yes Massa. I learning."

"That's kind of you, Luc," Philippe said. "He's been badly treated by his former master. Trust is what he needs."

"I don't hold with slavery," Luc assured him, "no matter what the colour of the skin."

Jonas learned well and quickly and the praise Luc showered on him seemed to make him grow in stature and well-being. Some days later, wakened at dawn by a constant murmuring outside, Philippe opened the door. There was Jonas in his strange mix of English and French, scolding the goat for trying to chew through his rope. Philippe was comforted. Jonas had made the animals his friends and found a place to feel at home.

They all had their chores to do. When Gaby's ankle had healed, she threw herself into an orgy of cleaning and baking. And, it was she who fed the chickens but Jonas gathered the eggs, holding each one like a precious jewel.

"Gaby," Luc called to her one morning, "I'd like you to look at these." He stood beside a sturdy wooden chest in a corner of the cabin. As he opened it, Gaby saw clothes neatly folded, lady's items on one side, baby's on another.

Luc saw her hesitation. "It's alright, Gaby. I'd like you to use them for making new clothes for your little ones or patching the old, whatever you wish." He saw her gazing with wonder at a dress that lay on top of the other clothing. He drew it out and handed it to her. "Try it on. Madeleine was just your size."

She went to the small scullery to change. The dress, flowing to the floor in a cascade of rose pink, with tiny white ruffles at neck and wrist, was fit for a princess and Gaby looked like one.

"Oh, Luc! Thank you! Thank You!" Then she saw his eyes wet with tears. She rushed to take his hands. "I'm sorry, Luc! I'm so sorry." Her own eyes were brimming.

"That was her wedding dress. She made it herself." He found it difficult to speak. "Madeleine would be pleased."

The mood was broken almost at once, by a crow of delight from Simon. Standing on tiptoe, he had found a treasure in the chest, a hand-carved wagon, complete with horse and driver.

"And here's something for Aimée," Luc said quietly and drew out an appealing rag doll made from flour sacks. "And we'll leave them to it, Philippe and Jonas, while we cut firewood and see if we can clear more land."

The three of them worked well together, the scent of the forest all around them. "At one time," Luc said, "we had to cut logs to send across the bay by schooner."

"For firewood?" asked Philippe.

"Oh no, to use in the fortifications. They were always in

need of repairs because of the salt, wind and weather."

Philippe remembered his hole in the crumbled wall and was thankful. "Where did you come from to settle here, Luc?" he asked.

"From Brittany. My wife and I came with a number of others from the same village."

What had happened to the others? Philippe didn't ask. He knew it was painful for Luc to speak of his wife. He was reminded of that a few days later when he and Jonas went to work on some trees beyond the barn. "Look, Massa," Jonas said, "A fence."

A wooden one, yes, and beyond it two crosses, one larger than the other. Jonas stared.

"Luc's wife and the baby he lost," Philippe said.

Jonas dropped to his knees and mumbled a prayer, unintelligible in a mixture of French and English. Philippe felt impelled to kneel beside him to bless the site silently.

One day as he and Jonas were cutting small branches to feed the fire, Philippe noticed a narrow path. Where did that go? Luc had not mentioned it but it looked well-trodden. Perhaps it was a private place where Luc had made a grotto to the Virgin Mary in memory of his wife and child. But why down a forest path? Why not close to his home? Perhaps there was an especially beautiful glade there. He tried not to think of other possibilities. Even after so many days of safety, he was still on the alert, not fully recovered from the anxieties of the forest trail.

Several days later the answer came. They had just finished breakfast and Philippe and Jonas were about to go out to tend the animals when Luc spoke. "We'll go along the trail when you've finished."

"For more wood?" Philippe asked.

"No, to Gull Cove. It's a fairly long hike so Gaby can tuck a little bread and cheese in a bag for you." He responded to the question in Philippe's eyes. "There's an abandoned settlement there. Several families came some time after we did and tried to fish and farm."

"What happened? Sickness? Disease?" Philippe asked.

"No, they felt they were too far from supplies. They moved closer to the fortress."

"And you, Luc?"

"I always felt with the wars between French and British the fortress could be attacked again. It was safer here. Once in a while a schooner comes by with supplies. Apart from that I provide my own."

"Then what's at Gull Cove?"

"A few cabins in ruins and one not so bad as the others," he paused, "with a new resident."

Philippe's heart quickened. "A newcomer here then?"

"A wayfarer, seeking shelter."

Gaby said, surprised. "A wayfarer in this lonely place? With a battle across the bay?"

"Where did he come from?" Philippe asked.

"Somewhere along the coast. He was in a terrible state when he got here. I didn't question him. He's running away from something. Maybe he lost his family in the battle and didn't want to be taken by the British."

His father? Long dormant, Philippe's hopes leaped.

Maybe his identity had been discovered and he'd had to take flight. Maybe.

Luc looked puzzled. "What is it, Philippe?"

Philippe shrugged. "Nothing of importance. You're probably right, and who could blame him for running away from all the fighting and suffering, looking for a new life and safety? That's what we're doing ourselves."

"I've been trying to help him with food from my own larder and tools to get him started on a little farm."

"Perhaps others will come and join him after the battle," Gaby said hopefully.

The more Philippe thought of it the more possible it seemed that it could be his father. If he couldn't reach the British he'd have had to leave the fortress to escape capture and death, and plan to join them later, after the victory. He tried not to sound too eager. "You can carry more to him with Jonas and me to help."

Luc agreed.

The day was typical of that coast, starting out with brilliant July sunshine, and by mid-morning, squalls of beating rain. But they were well protected by the trees. "And we can always dry out by Claude-Pierre's fire," Luc assured them.

Claude-Pierre? As good a name as any for his father to clothe his identity.

They smelled the smoke, hanging heavily on the damp air, even before they saw it issuing from the dwelling almost overtaken by the forest. Philippe's heart beat furiously as they approached the broken door. Could his search be over?

He was so startled when the door opened that he staggered back against Jonas. The fisherman at the door was the deserting soldier, the one they'd met at the limekiln. That square rugged face with the scar and piercing blue eyes were unmistakeable. He saw the alarm on the man's face. The soldier did not see the disappointment on his own.

Beckoning to the others, Luc entered the cabin. "More supplies, Claude-Pierre, and two new friends."

"Yes?" The man stepped back, eyeing Philippe as he would a dangerous animal.

Philippe overcame his emotion, and reached to shake his hand. "We're refugees, too, from the battle, Claude-Pierre, and Jonas, from a cruel master. I'm sure you'll make him welcome."

An understanding passed between them. "You're all welcome here. Come and dry yourselves." Claude-Pierre's voice shook a little. "I can give you some hot soup before you go back."

Luc eyed him with concern, "Are you ill, Claude-Pierre?"

"No! Oh, no, not at all! I've been wondering how I can make a new life here. I know so little about farming."

But Philippe thought he saw shame in the man's eyes. "Jonas and I would be glad to help you clear more land or rebuild your home, now we know the way here."

"For that I give you thanks." Claude-Pierre's voice still trembled.

"Monsieur," Philippe spoke firmly, "have no regrets. We've all had to put our lives behind us and start again. With the battle going so badly, you're better off here, especially if the fortress falls." And who was he to judge a deserting soldier when his own father was a spy?

Claude-Pierre cast him a grateful glance. "And what happens if the fortress does fall?"

"Make no mistake about that," Luc said. "The British will burn it to the ground."

"And what about us?" Claude-Pierre asked.

"I doubt they'll bother with the little outports and settlements. It was the fortress they feared. It's a threat to their trading lanes and their colonies in New England and Acadia." Luc went to fetch some bowls. "Come now. Let's have that soup and then we'll all do a little work on the clearing since the rain has let up."

Philippe ate without appetite. It was the last chance to find his father. It had all looked so promising. Now all his hopes were dashed. All he could do was give help where it was needed and pray, as Gaby did every night, for an answer to their future. And the soldier? Good luck to him. It would be a lonely life whoever won the battle.

Shadows

"The attack goes on." Philippe and Luc were drifting slowly on the bay before dawn in the dory, the net cast over the side.

"More fiercely than ever, I think." Luc gazed at the far horizon. "It looks as if the entire fortress is surrounded by shelling."

"It was a beautiful town." British though he was, Philippe felt a great sadness, as if the fortress had been part of his own life. In a way it had.

"What must be, must be." Luc noted his sadness. "Praise God for your little family's safety." He hauled in the net. "And for four fat cod to feed them! When you've breakfasted you can go gather more marsh hay for the cattle. There's some ready to cut and dry."

"Anything to help." But Philippe knew Luc was trying to take his mind from the battle. It was then he thought he saw, from the dory, a thin column of smoke rising above the trees. Who could have built a fire in the forest? So far from the fortress? As he looked the smoke dissolved in the air. A wisp of fog then, that was all. He said nothing as they rowed back to shore and the morning meal.

Following the grace and blessing, which Gabrielle offered before every meal, in the forest or out, Jonas went to clean out the barn. Philippe set off for the marsh.

He had scarcely gained the shelter of the densely growing trees when he thought he saw a figure flitting among them. *What kind of tricks was his imagination playing on him?* The shadows of uncertainty and fear took too long to die. He strode on through the trees, heading for the marsh. Then he saw a strange mound in a glade of trees he was passing. He went closer to examine it. What an odd formation to find in the midst of a wild forest! A burial mound, perhaps, but the arrangement of stones puzzled him. They seemed to be laid in some kind of design, too ornate for a cross, covering the entire top of the mound. It reminded him of something but even when he knelt to examine the design more closely, he couldn't think what it was.

It looked almost like a heraldic design that might have decorated a ship's banner on the day of Festival of St. Louis, as Gaby had described it. It could even be the symbol of some monastic order. Did Luc come to worship here? He wouldn't ask, that would be an invasion of Luc's privacy. Nonetheless, he wondered.

The next morning, he plunged into the work of cutting the hay and binding it to carry it back to dry at the clearing. He made several trips, stopping to give a word of encouragement to Jonas, who was spreading the ripe hay close to the barn. The mound in the glade occupied his thoughts, but he was reluctant to broach the subject to Luc. His puzzlement deepened the next day, when he returned to the marsh for more of the hay. His shoulders were bowed with the bundles. When one dropped and he bent to pick it up, a fragment of brown cloth, snagged on a tree bark, caught his eye. Part of a man's cloak? He pulled the piece from the tree and fingered it. The cloth was coarse, hand woven, the wearer not one of the wealthy then. Could it have been cloth from Madame Gabon's skirt or shawl? At the midday meal, his curiosity got the better of him. He took a deep breath and, àpropos of nothing that had been said before, suddenly turned to his host. "Luc, is there a place of worship here?"

"Only at the hearthside on my knees." Luc was puzzled by the sudden question. "There are small missions in the out-ports but they're all faraway from us." He gazed at Philippe anxiously. "Do you feel in need of a priest, lad?"

"Oh, no! No!" Philippe wished he'd never asked, grateful for the distraction caused by Aimée splashing a spoonful of rabbit stew over Simon's smock. Simon began to howl. Aimée took up the chorus and by the time peace was restored the subject of worship was forgotten. Philippe determined he would not mention it again.

When he returned to the marsh in the afternoon to finish the cutting he went to stand by the mound once more to try to make sense of the stone design. It would have been more evident if the stones had been smaller. But they were a mix-ture of sizes, obviously brought from the beach and carefully laid to cover the entire mound. As he stood staring, he had again the odd prickle at the nape of his neck. Someone was watching him, he knew it. He turned swiftly. Was that a move-ment just as swift beyond the open glade? Or was it his imagi-nation? Was it someone coming to the mound?

Gabrielle wondered at his silence at supper. "Philippe, are you ill? Have you been working too hard?"

Luc saved him from answering. "Hauling hay is hard work. We'll leave the rest for now — there will be fog, soon, and that will make the hay damp. Stay around the cabin for a while or do a bit of weeding in the garden."

That night, crawling wearily beneath the coarse bed sheet, he found sleep would not come. The mound in the forest haunted him. Dozing fitfully, he woke just before dawn, determined to explore the site again before the others wakened.

"Philippe!" Gaby had heard him. "Where are you going?"

"It's just something I have to see to, Gaby."

He left quickly before she was fully awake. Tripping over roots and fallen trees, he managed to find his way to the marsh and glade, even in the fog that Luc had predicted. Then suddenly he fell headlong, crashing into the undergrowth, but with the presence of mind to keep the torch from slipping from his hand. What was it that had blocked his path? He lowered the torch to see in the fog. A body! He had stumbled over a body! Just as he had Antoine's! But this was a young woman, her long fair hair matted and unkempt, her dress and brown cloak in rags. Was she living or dead? He knelt closer. He saw her torn blouse rise and fall with the slightest movement. Alive then! She was alive! But not just sleeping. No touch of his disturbed her. She was unconscious, from exhaustion, from lack of food and water. He must rouse the others, get help! He raced back to the cabin, in his haste stumbling and falling a dozen times.

Gaby was sitting up waiting for him.

"Gabrielle, Luke, Jonas! I need you." The others woke, dazed and confused, as he crashed in the door.

"It's a girl," he gasped, "a young woman! She's unconscious!"

"Where?" Luc didn't question him as to what he was doing up so early.

"We must help!" Gaby was grabbing for clothes. "Jonas, stay and watch the babies."

With a second torch, lit by Luc, they followed Philippe, Gaby with a blanket over her shoulder for the stranger. When they came to her, taking only a moment to stare at the still form, they lifted her tenderly on to the blanket and carried her carefully back to the cabin.

Jonas had the fire roaring and watched, wide-eyed, as they laid her before it.

"Water!" Gaby ordered. "We must force some water into her mouth. Then I'll take off her rags and dress her in my own clothes."

It was half an hour before the girl stirred and opened her eyes. They grew wide with puzzlement.

"You're safe. It's all right. Nothing can happen to you now." Gaby touched her tenderly. "You must take soup broth, a little at a time. I think you're starving."

The girl did as she was told, staring more in wonder than in fear, at all the faces ringed round her.

"We must find out who she is," Philippe said, "and why she's here. It's only then we can really help her."

"That will wait," Luc decided. "She needs a natural sleep now. We'll lay her on your mattress, Gaby."

"I'll stay to comfort her if she wakes," Gaby decided. "Jonas can watch with me."

And it was Jonas who spoke first when they came in from

the barn. "I knowing," he whispered. "I knowing."

Philippe drew closer. "You know who this is, Jonas?"

"I seeing her at the wharf. I seeing."

"Do you know her name?"

"No name, her father big man, fisherman. I seeing many times."

With the ongoing conversation all the others awoke, the little ones crying for food and attention. Gaby let them cry, kneeling over the girl to judge her condition. The girl tried to open her eyes but didn't speak. All day she kept her silence, but willingly accepted the food and drink Gaby offered.

"She's young and she'll regain her strength quickly," Gaby said.

She must have been wandering the forest for many days because it was several more before she stood strongly and did small tasks to help Gaby. But she said not a word.

"She'll come to it in time," Luc said. "She's had a terrible experience and we mustn't force her. Tomorrow we'll take some of Gaby's bread and soup to our new neighbour. The walk in the forest with us to protect her will help banish her fears."

The day began with fog but it had burned off by mid-morning and their procession through the trees was accompanied by birdsong and the wash of waves on the rocky shore. Claude-Pierre was nowhere in sight as they left the forest. Then they heard the ring of an axe beyond the cabin. "We'll follow the sound," Luc said. "He'll be there clearing more ground."

He was. He turned as they called. For a moment only he said nothing. Then he caught sight of the girl. His voice was a shout of wonderment and joy. "Jeanne! Jeanne! My Jeanne!" He rushed to embrace her.

"Claude-Pierre!" The cry broke the girl's silence at last.

The children were screaming at all the excitement and between endearments exchanged by the lovers, Luc managed to get them all into the house. There he built up the fire to dispel the dampness and made them all quieten and sit around it on the floor, while they ate large portions of Gaby's bread smothered with her preserves.

"And now," Luc said, reaching out and taking Jeanne's hand in his own, "it's time for you to tell us your story."

It was told haltingly, with many a cherishing glance between the lovers. Claude-Pierre had asked Jeanne to marry him, but her father forbade the marriage.

"He said with a battle on, I could be a widow within a week!" Jeanne said. "I was too frightened to argue with him. I knew if I did, he'd punish me and lock me in my room."

"So how did you escape?" Philippe asked.

"Jacques spoke to me after Claude-Pierre had got away safely."

"He told me he was going to try to persuade you," Claude-Pierre told her. "But I didn't think he had a hope." He gazed at her as if he still couldn't believe his eyes. "How did he manage it?"

"He said how wonderful it would be for us to start a new life in one of the outports. He waited for me at midnight in the alley that runs behind our house and we made it to the hole in the wall and he helped me through." She seemed suddenly overcome with emotion.

"And then?" Luc asked gently.

"He told me to look for Claude-Pierre at the old limekiln, but I couldn't find it. I ran out of all the food I'd taken from the larder and got weaker and weaker. I tried to follow the sound of the sea so I wouldn't get lost."

"Just as we did," Gaby said.

Anxiety was etched on Claude-Pierre's face. "And what happened to my old friend, Jacques?"

"He didn't make it! He didn't, and it's all my fault." Jeanne broke into a torrent of sobbing.

Holding her close, Claude-Pierre tried to comfort her. "Maybe he got out later. He could still come."

"He'll never come! Not now! He said it was better not to go together and while he was seeing me safely away from the wall, they shot him. One of our own soldiers! They must have thought he was British!" Jeanne clung to Claude-Pierre. "And it was all because of me!"

"God and the Holy Mother bless his soul!" Claude-Pierre, too, found it hard to hold back his tears. The others, realizing the sacrifice, were silent.

Luc spoke quietly. "He would be happy to know you are safe, Jeanne. Take comfort in that. There'll be many deaths before this is over. And we must make plans for this couple, happy plans faraway from the fighting."

"What plans can we make?" Gaby asked. "You have no chapel near."

"No, but a priest from Fourchu comes by boat now and then to administer the sacraments, and to see how we're doing." He smiled at Claude-Pierre and Jeanne. "The next time he can administer the sacrament of marriage."

"A wedding!" Gaby hugged Jeanne. "Oh, we'll have a fine time getting ready for it! And Jeanne can share our home until he comes!"

"A happy ending in the midst of war," Luc said. "May God bless us all!"

A happy ending! And where is ours? Philippe wondered. And then was ashamed of his lack of joy and gratitude for the young couple's good fortune.

Luc was calling them all to follow him home for a celebration in honour of the two young lovers.

Journey into Darkness

Father Armac arrived within the week bringing the latest news of the siege. The town was being shelled from all directions. "They've even called in some of the sailors from the ships to help in the land defence."

Luc, anxious, leaned towards him. "Father, what about the rest of the French fleet?"

"Beaten back by the force of British strength. The frigate Arethuse was very brave and effective on the front line but she's had to withdraw for repairs."

"And what of the hospital and the citadel, Father?" Gaby asked. "Are they safe?"

"Nothing is safe now in the fortress, dear child. A shell exploded in the courtyard of the citadel and another in the hospital itself, killing a surgeon and wounding two Brothers of Charity. Let us pray for all those under threat of war."

They knelt around him, each thanking God silently for safety and for whatever the future held. There was a long silence broken only by the crackling of the fire. Then Philippe sprang to his feet. "Father, we have a joyful occasion here. The sacrament of marriage! You've arrived at a blessed time for us!"

Gaby hastened to explain, omitting the details of Claude-Pierre's background and telling only how Jeanne, to find him, had come on a journey fraught with danger. "And we've even made her a wedding gown from Madame Gabon's wardrobe and my own bits and pieces. It'll all be beautiful!"

And it was. They made an altar in a bower among the nearer trees and decorated it with wild iris. "My wife's favourite flower," Luc told them.

Gaby had pressed some items of Luc's clothing so that Claude-Pierre could be as dashing a groom as circumstances permitted. Jeanne was a lovely bride, wildflowers crowning her hair and filling her bouquet. The sun, making its fitful appearance from behind a bank of clouds, shone on them all quite suddenly. No one thought to hush the children's screams of joy as they played. Jonas, whose role had been explained to the priest, knelt in awe some distance from them and the ceremony.

"Now for the wedding feast!" Gaby announced. "I've done the best I can!" Her best was a delight to the eye and the tongue. Roast venison, vegetables from the garden and a wedding cake sweetened with wild honey. They all ate as if there were no tomorrow.

They watched Jeanne and Claude-Pierre go hand in hand down the forest trail to begin a new life together. Then, kneeling on the shore, they received a final blessing from Father Armac and waved and waved until his small boat was out of sight.

Luc went to tend the animals, Jonas at his heels. Gaby and Philippe, alone on the beach, stared at the retreating dory and the far distant shore.

"And what will become of us?" Gaby spoke quietly.

For a moment Philippe said nothing. The joy and excitement of the wedding over, he felt bereft and anxious. "For now we're safe, that's what we wanted." *But I wanted to find my father, he thought.*

Gaby sensed his feelings. "Philippe, I'm truly grateful to you for bringing us to Luc's, but you came to Isle Royale to find your father."

He took her hands in both his own. "But I found you," he said, his gaze warm and loving. "And we're grateful to Luc for making us welcome, even if we are rather a strange family." *And a family they were now, he knew. But, what will happen when the fortress falls to the British? Shall we be here then?* Aloud he said cheerfully. "I think Luc likes our company. It's helped him to get over his loss. He's smiling more these days and he's put on weight with your good cooking." He looked thoughtful. "Gaby, were slaves ever set free in Louisbourg?"

She knew what troubled him. "Not children. But one slave became an apprentice baker and a citizen bought the freedom of a girl slave and married her. God will look after Jonas. We'll just have to leave the future to Him. I pray about it every night." Her hand still clasping Philippe's, she turned back to the cabin.

An answer came sooner than either one of them could have imagined. A week passed with constant work, tending the animals and the garden and helping Luc to clear more land. With occasional visits from Jeanne and Claude-Pierre, they were secure in their companionship and all thrived on the simple abundant food.

"Time for picking more wild mushrooms." Philippe announced one morning. "The fog and rain have lifted. It's a good day." He didn't mention the continuing lightning blaze of battle below the far horizon. They were always aware of that.

He went first, as if drawn by an unseen hand, to stand at the mound where the stones made such a strange design. He had decided never to mention it to Luc in case it did involve some secret. He took one last look, then plunged deeper into the forest where the wild fungus was plentiful.

He heard the slight sound before he knew the reason for it. Not another fugitive! Oh, please God, not that! He stared at the trees, then he knew it was not all trees before him. One was a tall figure, whose gray-brown robe could hardly be distinguished from them. The figure did not move. Philippe stared at it silently, willing it to speak. Then he caught a quick glimpse of the face almost concealed beneath the hooded cowl. The face stared back with one eye. One eye! That could only mean one person! The Monk! The Monk had come to find them, not in his usual ghostly white robe but in one that made him invisible in the forest!

"Good Brother! Oh, Good Brother, you've found us!"

The words the Monk spoke came in a strange strangled voice as if there were no room for them to escape. *Was this the damage that had been done to him?* Philippe shook his head and moved closer. "Good Brother, I can't understand. Please speak more slowly."

"Gabrielle and the babies, where are they?"

"Safe, Good Brother, and the slave, Jonas, too." Then he held his breath. *After all, what did he really know of the Monk? He, too, might be a spy, come to betray them. He had no doubt the Monk had guessed he was British.*

His doubts were dispelled by the Monk's next tortured words. Philippe had to strain to understand them. "The end of the fortress is near. I can help you escape before it falls."

Escape! What a beautiful word! But Philippe said nothing. Could he believe this strange man? Was it some trick he had up his sleeve? But then, how good he'd been to Gaby and the children, and even to himself! He mustn't lose faith. "Good Brother, I'm waiting to know how." The Monk had not moved but Philippe shortened the distance between them, waiting.

"The *Aréthuse*," the Monk paused, every hoarse word an effort. "She's going to break through the barricade and sail for France."

"Father Armac told us of the *Arethuse*, but what does she have to do with us?"

"You must all come with me."

"To where?"

The Monk paused for breath, his words even more distorted when he spoke. "To a small cove, where a dory is hidden. I'll take you to the *Arethuse*. We must go at once. There is no time to waste."

"But, Monsieur! The British fleet! They'll be on guard!"

"I know the way I shall take. We'll wait for night and the fog. I have friends on the French ships watching. We have signals." His voice broke as it attempted to rise. "Go now. Fetch the others!"

Philippe turned and ran, spilling his basket of mushrooms on the trail. He shouted to Luc and Jonas working in the clearing and burst into the cabin.

Gaby started up in alarm. "What is it? Has something happened? Luc? Jonas? Are they hurt?"

The two barged in the door to answer her question. "We're here, Gaby," Luc said. "Philippe, is there new danger?"

Philippe was breathless. "There will be danger but perhaps escape." He turned to Gaby. "The Monk is at the edge of the forest, waiting. There's a ship preparing to run the blockade and sail for France. He wants us to be on it!"

"But how …?"

"No time for questions, Gaby. We must gather up the babies and some clothing and be gone at once."

But Jonas had covered his face with his hands. "Oh, Massa! No ship! No ship for Jonas!"

Philippe knew why. A ship was small, with few places to hide. On board, Jonas would be a slave again, and he had heard of the beatings inflicted on slaves by cruel captains. As Jonas cried out, Luc spoke. "The boy will stay here. He can run the farm with me and be my companion. Let anyone try to harm him, and he will have to deal with me. As I told you, I don't hold with slavery."

Jonas knelt at his feet. "Oh, Massa, thank you. Thank you! Oh, Massa!"

Luc lifted him gently. "There'll be no more of that, Jonas." He smiled. "You're more help to me on your feet than on your knees."

Gaby reached out to take Luc's hand. "But what of you, Luc? You'll be so alone when we're gone! What of you?"

"We have Jeanne and Claude-Pierre down the trail and

I've no doubt when the affair at the fortress is over there'll be new settlers from the old countries. The cod will bring them if nothing else, and we'll have families here again. And Jonas and I shall be happy knowing you're safe."

Safe! If only Philippe knew they would be! But there was no time to be anxious. "Hurry, Gaby. Bundle up the babies' clothes and as little as we can do with. I saw the Monk's carryall. He'll have all the supplies we need for the journey."

They were ready too quickly. As they moved to the door, Luc turned and withdrew something from the wooden chest in the corner. "Philippe, I want you to have this. It's the only thing of value I have to give."

Stunned, Philippe gazed at the gift. It was a leather bookmark, the design of a family crest tooled in gold on its surface. The shock was so great, he could hardly stand upright. Then he knew where he had seen the design attempted on the stone mound in the forest. It was his mother's family crest. He hardly needed to be told the rest.

"It was in the pocket of a man in fisherman's clothes. After a terrible gale last September, his body washed up on the shore some distance from here. I caught sight of it when I was coming back from dawn fishing and brought him home in my boat. This must have been a treasured possession."

Oh, it was! It was! His mother had given it to his father as a bookmark for his Bible as he left on his mission. At last, Philippe had found his father. Luc looked puzzled at Philippe's silence. "I gave him a proper burial with prayers and blessings," he assured them. "He lies deep in the forest, his grave covered with stones to keep the wild animals away."

Oh, yes, I know, I know! But there was no time to explain. Aloud Philippe said, "Luc, dear Luc." He tried to still the tremble in his voice. "I shall treasure this forever. Forever and ever."

The farewells were said in a shower of tears and swift embraces. As they raced up the knoll, Philippe looked back. Luc stood quite still, clasping Jonas's small hand in his own. Philippe gave them a fond salute, then, resolutely, putting the past behind him, sped with Gaby, the babies on their backs, into the darkness of the forest.

"Fair blows the wind for France!"

The Monk's way through the forest was sure, even if they travelled in darkness or fog. He seemed to know by instinct or experience all the trails made by animals or woodcutters. The going was made almost easy for Gaby and Philippe, as the Monk strode ahead, one child in his arms, the other on his back.

"How wonderful there was enough of the sleeping draught left over to keep them quiet," Gaby whispered.

Philippe nodded. "We'll need it more than ever as we get closer to the fortress and the ships."

The Monk spoke for the first time on their journey, his fractured voice hardly a whisper above the crackle of the night fire. "When we reach the harbour, there must be silence. The *Aréthuse* knows we're coming. She's left the careening dock repaired. We have to make our way through some of the British ships before we meet her."

Gaby's voice trembled. "But how shall we find her in the fog, Good Brother?"

"I've studied the configuration of both fleets. We've arranged signals by lantern." That was all. They were both comforted with his assurance.

There was one more word from him, one only. They had stopped after a long day's scramble over underbrush and through tough thickets. A stream burbled nearby as they sat by the fire, devouring with great hunger, the meat, cheese and bread from the Monk's haversack. Fed and comforted, the children slept rolled in blankets on spruce boughs. Gaby, almost asleep herself with exhaustion, grabbed Philippe's arm.

"What? What's the matter?"

"Look! Up there on the branch, almost over our heads!"

Eyes! Slits of eyes gleaming in the firelight, staring at them. Alarmed, Philippe reached out to protect her.

The Monk's whisper came quickly. "Cougar!" He clapped his hands loudly and the eyes were gone.

Their uncertainty was not so easily dispelled when, in the dark, they arrived at a little cove where a dory was waiting. There was a strange, forbidding quiet over all. In the fog the bombardment had ceased. There was only the sound of waves on the shore. A sudden screaming made Philippe clutch Gaby's hand more tightly. Then the flutter of wings. Gulls, disturbed in their night resting-place. The sleeping children, still wrapped in the blankets, were placed in the bottom of the boat. Philippe helped Gaby to a place beside him and behind the Monk who took up his place on the thwart, the oars in his hands.

Fraught with danger, the strange journey began. The Monk must have had a map of the British ships in his mind's eye. He rowed unerringly among them, so close at times Philippe could have reached out to touch a wooden hull. It seemed the lights on the enemy ships themselves, unearthly halos in the fog, were what guided him, as he rowed, sometimes among wreckage caused by the French shells.

There was a sudden bump against the dory's stern. Gaby peered into the water, her eyes wide with horror. The body of a French sailor floated behind them.

But this is war, thought Philippe. *There'll be more bodies, French and British both, before we finish this journey.* He said nothing but he was right. For them, there was more danger than from bodies in the water.

Into the stillness came disembodied voices.

"Who goes there?"

"What is it, mate?"

British ships! English voices!

"I heard something!"

"You're imagining things, Harry. Easy on a night like this!"

"Listen, Tom! It's the dip of oars!"

The Monk stilled them at once. They all sat waiting, not daring to breathe.

"I don't hear a thing, Harry. What fool fisherman would be out on a night like this?"

Then Simon, drugged though he was, whimpered.

"There! Did you hear that? Somebody's out there, I tell you!"

"Only a seabird of some kind, Harry. The ships and the battle have disturbed all their nests."

"You sure?"

"Sure as I am we'll be at it again tomorrow. Come on mate, we're off watch now. Let's go and wake Will and Ed to get on up here." Their voices mumbled into the dark and distance on the ship.

Quickly the Monk took up the oars again and silently

plied their way past the danger. It was then Philippe saw the two lanterns winking at the stern of each ship they passed.

The French fleet! They must be among them! The captains were making a corridor for them to traverse to safety. He felt a great burden lift from his heart. He thought suddenly of the strange round grave in the forest at Gabarus. Surely his father would want him to do this, to rescue Gaby and the children and take them to his grandmother's home.

Then he saw the three lanterns! *Three! A special signal!* Had they arrived at the *Aréthuse*? He listened. There were whispers high on the deck, in French. The Monk drew the dory alongside and pointed. Slowly a rope ladder slipped noiselessly over the gunwale. It came to rest against the dory. As they watched in silence, a French sailor came swiftly down the ladder, took Simon on one arm and clambered to the deck with the other. In a moment he was back for Aimée, cradling her more tenderly against his body. Perhaps he had one such baby at home, Philippe thought. But then it was Gaby's turn, half a dozen hands waiting to help her on to the deck.

Philippe was the last. How could he leave the Monk without words of gratitude? But there was no time. He saw a flash of scarlet and a cross beneath the Monk's cowl and then he was hauled up the ladder before he could speak.

As he joined the others, he was blessed by a Récollet friar, the ship's chaplain. When he looked down the Monk and the dory had gone. Gone forever from his life.

"God keep him in the battle!" Gaby spoke her blessing aloud.

"Aye, Mademoiselle, and all of us as we make our getaway." A lieutenant, his eyes half closed with sleep, had come on deck. "The Monk brought you?"

"He did," Philippe said. "Do you know him?"

"We came from the same village in France. He arranged all this with me at the careening wharf while we were in for repairs."

Gaby stared at the babies asleep on the deck. "With this terrible battle going on, he saved all our lives."

"Not only yours, Mademoiselle. In the siege of '45 he rescued a young sailor from death and was slashed across the throat. That's why he seldom speaks."

And why he wears the cowl. Aloud Philippe said, "And what happened to the young sailor?"

The lieutenant smiled. "He's standing here before you. The Monk was honoured by the King. He's a chevalier of the Order of St. Louis!"

Perhaps that was the scarlet ribbon and cross Philippe had caught sight of as the Monk helped him aboard ship. A brave and wonderful chevalier.

"Come now." The lieutenant bent to pick up Simon. "Bring the other baby, Michel." He spoke to a very young fair-haired midshipman. "You know the cabin set aside for them to rest from their journey. See that they're looked after."

They made their way past coils of rope and barrels of ammunition. In the cabin they were brought food and water and made comfortable on makeshift bunks and beds. Gaby, overcome with exhaustion, was asleep in an instant, her arms around the children.

Philippe whispered to Michel. "So we're going to run the blockade?"

"Within the hour."

"But how will we ever do it?"

"With the best and bravest captain in the French fleet, Captain Vauquelin. He fought a brilliant battle against the British fleet as long as he could. He'll get us through if anyone can. The fog's our blessed friend. And we've all prayed to St. Nicholas for a safe journey." Michel drew Philippe to a straw mattress. "Young monsieur, lie down before you drop. Leave everything to us, and sleep."

Philippe lay down and tried to stay awake. *What if the attempt to run the blockade failed? What if they were captured by the British? What would his role be then?* As he lay, determined to keep alert, he felt the ship tremble and heard the grating ratch of the anchor rising inch by inch. He tried to listen for whispered commands but his exhaustion was too great. The constant fear for his little family, the long, arduous trek to the cove, the suspense aboard the dory, overcame him. He slept.

He woke with a start. Gaby was shaking him. "Philippe! Shots! I heard guns! What shall I do with the babies?"

Wide awake now, he heard the noise of gunfire above the shudder of canvas and the creak of the rigging. "The British. They're giving chase. We'll get away! Don't be afraid." *But would they?* He sat holding her close for her comfort and his own. The sporadic exchanges of gunfire seemed to go on forever. Then just as suddenly it stopped.

"They've given up. We'll be safe!" Unless another ship

took up the chase. But only the sounds of the *Aréthuse* going about its own ship's business broke the night's foggy quiet.

In the silence, once again they fell deeply asleep, to the creak of lines, the shudder of canvas.

Philippe awoke and sat bolt upright. Where was he? At once he felt the movement of the great ship moving in the water. The sound of sailors' shouts, the wind whistling in the rigging. Had they made it? Were they safe? He was aware of a different light in the cabin. The sun! The sun was shining!

Michel appeared at the cabin door. He was grinning from ear to ear. "We've made it! We've got clean away! Didn't I tell you we had the cleverest captain in the French fleet?"

"We're safe?" Gaby wakened, her face creased with deep sleep. "Truly safe?"

"Truly safe, Mademoiselle. You'll need a wash-up and some food, but first come with me."

Still only half-awake, they stumbled after him.

"The sun's shining! The fog's almost gone!" Gaby's face itself shone.

They followed Michel to the stern of the ship. Faraway, on the horizon they saw the ruins of Louisbourg, great bursts of gunfire and shelling exploding in the wavering fog.

"The spires of Louisbourg are gone," Philippe said quietly.

"Forever, I think," Michel said. "Have you someone waiting for you, Monsieur?"

"My grandmother in Provence, Michel. Perhaps there will be spires, there, too." And certainly a welcome and love for them all, he knew that. As Gaby, tears in her eyes, turned away from the blaze of battle, he said softly. "Remember Gaby, a new life."

He knew, like him, she was remembering the Monk, Gros Raymond, Emilie and Antoine, Claude-Pierre and Raoul and the last swift glimpse of Luc and Jonas standing hand-in-hand on the shore.

But only he would remember, always, the mound, covered with stones in heraldic design, deep in a forest glade.

Suddenly a shout rang out. A sailor was perched high in the rigging, looking to the east. "The *Aréthuse* is on her way home! Fair blows the wind for France!"

Philippe drew Gaby close. His face mirrored his happiness. He looked up at the sails, full and billowing in the following wind. He echoed the sailor's joyful shout, "Fair blows the wind! Fair blows the wind for France!"